Aftermath: Boise Idaho

Ann Wuehler

POE BOY
PUBLISHING

PART ONE: THAT'S MY BLOOD

They'd found her. Hannah listened, sitting against the wall, three floors up, only the roof above her head and then the sky above that. Sunlight came in between the crusty blankets she had hung over the two windows and made pretty patterns on the filth and dust of the buckled floorboards. Who would put wooden flooring in? It seemed such a waste. Hannah ran her hand over that dull, gouged floor rather than listen to the sly fingers scraping on the outside of the door. She had her hockey stick, her hunting knife. Guns just made noise and needed ammo, as Lyle had joked not seven days before. Lyle who now lay in a heap of guts and broken splintery bones, with Jack one of the zombies now, his left arm eaten off but still zombie.

"Fucking go away," Hannah whispered, noting a dusty blue vase, embossed with one of those happy hobo clowns—something an old lady would buy in installments from a magazine like Lillian Vernon. It seemed fitting she would end her life with a broken clown vase. Lyle's death, Jack shambling about ... she'd had enough. Her hunting knife was dull and beating her own head in with a hockey stick seemed beyond her talents at the moment. She had not eaten for almost three days and that last tiny drop of rain had at least slaked her thirst a bit. No hope remained. No one else was alive. If they were, they were not in Boise, Idaho. This tiny apartment she had holed up in would be her tomb—hurray! By the time the zombies broke through the door, she'd be long dead and hopefully too putrid for them to munch. They liked fresh kills, they liked kills that still screamed and fought to get away even as they ripped them to pieces. Hannah had watched an hour-long nature show on hyenas, once upon a time. The hyenas ate their prey while it still kicked and squealed. She remembered that, staring at the door she had blocked with the stove, which she had somehow dragged over, before fainting from that bit of manual labor.

Yes, heavy breathing out there; the zombies listening. It was their world now, they were welcome to it.

Hannah fetched that vase and broke it. Sharp edges. Her mind settled low and peaceful. Cut from wrist to elbow. Cutting across the wrist was wrong. It took longer, it didn't cut the right veins, something like that. The zombies rattled the doorknob. She bit her lips, or giggles would have escaped her. Why were they trying the doorknob? Except... they seemed to know that a locked door meant human chow behind it. She didn't want to be alive when they managed to get into her hidey-hole. She didn't want to see them or smell them or feel their rotting hands on her cringing flesh.

The sharp ragged edge met her flesh, sank deep as she yanked it upward from the prominent veins of her wrist to the bend of her elbow. Blood, immediate and shocking; how it tickled, how it tickled. The drip of blood onto the dirty floor, the dimming of that faint light. Hannah settled back against the wall, and got her right hand to cut at her left arm until the blood tickled and tickled and tickled her skin. She watched her own blood pool and flow and turn colors as it picked up dirt and debris. The light dimming, fingers scrabbling on the other side of that door. She heard a fly buzzing against the glass of the window. She heard it and heard it and heard it. The pretty blood tickling her skin. The smell of her own blood, like hot raw pennies. Peace where no thoughts or fears could live. Her blood, that shard of blue vase in her right hand, coated with something red. *Why, that's my blood. Yes, it is.*

PART TWO: THE RUSTLE OF PAPERS

"Hannah? Hannah, wake up." A soft female voice in her ear, the rustle of papers, the typing one heard from laptops and computers and devices, the hum of bored voices, the ring of several phones. Hannah sat up at a corner desk, a computer before her, and a file open: letter/fundraiser/Halloween. Nothing yet written—not even a date or an address or anything. The blinking curser waiting for her to start the letter. A picture of her, with short fluffy hair, next to a tall man who looked like he had just stepped off a movie set. Someone had drawn a heart around her and that strange man.

A woman stood by Hannah as she struggled to wake up, wearing a sedate hunter green dress and a blue paisley scarf, her golden-brown hair in a sedate updo secured with a large barrette. "Late night? That letter needs to be finished by five. What are you doing? Get it finished."

Hannah blinked, looked around. She sat at the very back of a giant room full of other desks. Others working. Others. Behind her, a giant window overlooking a street; other tall buildings, trees. She wore dark brown slacks, a light raspberry-colored sweater, and a fake string of pearls! No zombies that she could tell. What was this? No. No, be smart, be careful. "Yes, late night. Do you think you can help me with this letter?"

"Oh, well, sure." The woman pulled over a chair, sat, smelling of peaches. Peach perfume or peach shampoo. Something faint yet pleasant. Everything in this office—a big wide space of many desks with mostly women working at them — seemed very clean. "Jodi wants two points hit, right? It's for a good cause and you can win prizes. Keep it the same bullshit as always, is my advice. Fectos don't like change. They like order and things to go a certain way. Jodi should run everything here, she's so wonderfully organized."

Fectos? Hannah looked at the calendar on the desk. It said September. But what day? What year? "Oh sure, Fectos don't like change. Jodi's so organized, sure."

"No, they sure don't like change! They like tradition and order. Who doesn't? Jodi says tradition and order win every time, no matter what. It always comes back to tradition and order." Why did the peach-smelling office drone seem so stuck on this Jodi? "God, Lana at the meeting this morning! I about choked on my coffee. She's hell-bent on naming names, you know? You should avoid her. Not take rides from her. Or Phil." The woman had clear brown eyes. And an agenda. Mystery! It felt so nice to have such a harmless little mystery to solve as this woman and her office shenanigans. "Oh hey, just pull up that other fundraising crap from Christmas. Copy and paste what you need, slap a new date on it, change some details, there ya go! Do you still have them? It's what I do, for the updates. I just copy and paste, it's not like there's changes at our level. Oh hey, did you hear? The wall got breached over on the Oregon side. Eatery Fectos got through, it was a mess. Nora has to deal with that PR nightmare. She's in tears over it. Henry will probably fly up from Winnemucca if she fucks it up. And you know she will. And Henry will want to ... you know." The woman rolled her eyes as Hannah searched for a Christmas fundraising letter. There — a Christmas file and yes, a list of fundraising letters and events. The woman leaned forward a bit, nodded. "That one. Try that one, about the Holly Ball. That was the auction one, that's kind of like the Halloween thing for this year. Yep. Just copy and paste what you need. The Fectos like their auctions. But we're not supposed to know about the ones where they buy kids. Yuck. We all know about Salliana but we don't know, you know? Just copy and paste what you need. It's what we all do."

"Thank you. I seem to have lost my notes for this fundraiser. And the name. I so spaced off or something. Salliana, yeah, that's so gross," Hannah said with a giant goofy smile, her brain ticking away furiously. What the hell was all this? Was she in hell? Had she been sent to hell to write fundraiser letters? She did not have office experience of any kind. No magical spate of knowledge on office letter writing came to enlighten her, either.

"That's not like you. Are you okay? Is it Kevin?" The woman looked around, then leaned in, her breath reeking with coffee and spearmint gum. "Don't let that pretty boy distract you. Keep your eye on the prize. You know what happens if you get distracted here."

"Sure. Yeah, Kevin ... he's very distracting lately. We're fighting." Hannah said and the woman nodded. "So, it's the 19th today, right?"

"What is? Oh crap ... there's Jodi. Just get that done and sent to her. And no more napping. Maybe call in sick tomorrow. Kevin is not worth it. Don't fall apart now." The woman pushed the chair she had taken back into the empty desk beside Hannah's. She walked back up the aisle, toward a messy desk piled high with wrapped boxes. A woman in a navy silk pantsuit stopped to speak to her and at that point, Hannah noticed this navy pantsuit woman ... was a zombie. She moved slowly and carefully, she wore an obvious wig the color of moldy carrots. Hannah had the letter opener in her hand, which had a Bureau of Humans on its silver handle. Zombies. They were in hell, of course they were. She'd have to fight her way free... Why was no one else screaming and running? No one seemed to care an actual zombie moved among them, and the zombie seemed oddly intent on pretending to be a boss or a supervisor. And then that zombie shuffled toward Hannah and Hannah came to her feet, her bladder hot and heavy and ready to let go down her leg.

The sensation crawled down Hannah's spine that someone watched her. Studied her. Someone besides this zombie bitch about to ... to attack her, of course. That's what zombies did. They were famous for it.

"Hannah. Is that letter done yet? I need it." The zombie came right to Hannah's desk, stood there, oblivious to the fact that she was a zombie or that she should be trying to rip Hannah's face off. It was unnatural. This was an unnatural zombie. "Hannah?" There it was, that smell, masked only slightly by heavy floral fumes that someone had tried to perhaps label a perfume. Filmy gummy eyes, a light silvery veil actually worn, that hooked behind the droopy ears. *Maybe a Muslim zombie? Don't laugh, don't ask!*

"Fine. Good. About done." Hannah mumbled out, her voice tight and high. Jodi the zombie stared at her, then stepped closer as Hannah stepped back, the wall meeting her back, her hand a fist around that letter opener. Those gummy eyes went to the letter opener, then to Hannah's face.

"Is there a problem?" The voice, gritty and low; the voice of dead things that should not be speaking. "Did you and your boyfriend have a tiff?"

"No. Fine." Hannah made herself casually drop the letter opener, near an actual letter. "I'm fine. Fine."

"Uh huh. Please get that done in the next half an hour.

It should have been done this morning. Don't let cute boys distract you, dear."

"Fine." Hannah could not stop repeating that word. Cute boys? Had she heard that? "Today's date?"

"Yes, the nineteenth. Use the Winnemucca address at the top. We're including our whole territory this year. And the Boise one, of course. I'm pondering whether or not to extend to Salt Lake, but I can put in that address if I do, so don't worry about that. Thank you, Hannah. You're a good worker, and I know it will be done and well written. You manage to improve even a copy and paste job. Take Sunni as your model if you need guidance." Jodi moved off and Hannah sat slowly, then noticed she really had to go. Her bladder had turned into a throbbing monster. Bathroom. Or she'd squat and pee on the ugly dark gray carpet like a bad dog.

After a careful look about, she got up, wearing low heels that pinched her feet and pantyhose beneath her slacks. Pantyhose. That were a bit too small. Hannah walked up that aisle, trying not to gape at everything. It seemed everyone knew her and that she worked here. Wherever *here* was. A gigantic white square clock said it was past two. Afternoon, had to be afternoon. The sun shone through that big window. White walls. Insane asylum? Inside of a white whale?

"Hannah, instead of potato salad, can we go halvsies on a cheese and cracker tray?" a Mexican-looking woman said to her as she went past, heading toward the big glass double doors. Hannah stopped. "Jodi just said she's bringing her potato salad. We can't have two potato salads."

"Sure. Cheese and crackers." It seemed important to just agree with whatever was said to her. Food. There was food nearby yet her stomach did not seem empty. No raging thirst. No trots from sipping dirty water. It seemed there were bigger actual offices outside the glass doors, with nameplates screwed into them. Zombies lurched in and out of these offices ... wearing nice clothes. Zombies dressed up like bankers. God damn it.

"Han? Are you getting sick? You're pale," the woman said, tapping away at a laptop—some kind of numbers report. "You need a Skeezie?"

"Sure, yeah. A Skeezie."

The woman reached her hand into a desk drawer, her fingernails painted beige. Those beige-tipped fingers brought out a small opaque bag and this got handed to Hannah in a secretive way, rather like she was being handed a tampon. "Just take what you need! Take one right before you go home. Otherwise, you'll, well, you know." The woman made gusty wind sounds and waved her hands a bit, then laughed.

"Thanks, Susan," Hannah threw out and the woman snorted, then pulled up something else that had even tinier, insufferably smug, collections of numbers and columns.

"Okay, Betty."

Hannah saw a memo with the name Katherine at the top. "I'll just take one for later, Katherine."

"Katherine? What? Maybe you should take one now and just go home. Just put that bag in your top desk drawer, I'll get it later."

Another memo, with Ophelia on it. Damn it. Hannah was getting too unnerved and chickenshit to try another name. Then Ophelia, not Katherine, looked over at the woman who had helped Hannah with her fundraiser memo. "You're friends again with Sunni? After she hit on Kevin? You're a saint, Hannah. Though, you should let her have him. He's trouble."

Sunni, the woman in the hunter green granny dress. Okay. Jodi, the zombie. And now Ophelia. And Kevin, the man in the picture. Okay, got it. "I like trouble," said Hannah, her face trying to smirk. *No, no, you don't know these people or what's going on.* "Forgive and forget. Thanks for the Skeevers."

"Skeevies. Uh ... you want me to go with you?" Hannah wasn't fully listening. She was gawping at a very tall, gaunt zombie draped in an eye-watering poison yellow suit, paired with a blood-red tie. "What? Oh yeah, Harrison, he wore that yellow suit yesterday. He looks like a giant canary." Harrison spoke to Jodi, hands moving slowly, gray hands... He had gray hands. "Don't stare at them, they hate that. Fectos, they want us to pretend they're normal. He's such a perv. They all are. We're not supposed to notice. Or care."

"Yeah, Fectos. Fine." Hannah forced herself to walk through those glass double doors and walk past Jodi and the zombie canary man. She saw two restrooms — male and female and a unisex one — plus a break room, with the door open and two men seated at the big table, coffee cups before them, heads together. They nodded at her as she went past and she nodded back. Once in the ladies, she sat on a toilet, which had a bowl full of clear bright water. The air smelled of roses from the air freshener left by the third sink. She took deep, head-swirling breaths, trying to calm herself.

Off came her slacks, simple pull up ones, and then those damn pantyhose got torn off. She stuffed them in the little wastebasket, and covered them with toilet paper. Actual toilet paper — not leaves or her own hand. There were used tampons, wrapped in shielding layers, in there as well. When had she last had enough to eat to be able to shit something out? Or have her period? The little bag

Not-Katherine had handed her held six black pills. They were stamped with an S and were long pills, not round. The black coating smudged her fingers. Skeezies? Skeezers? Skeezawhatevers? She took one, put it into the pocket of her slacks. Then sat again, not ready yet to face going back out there.

Where the zombies were.

What was going on? What was that name the two women had used? Fecto. Festo? No, Fectos. Both had casually said it, as if they used that term for zombies all the time. What did it mean?

Someone came into the restroom, went into the next stall. A series of astonishing farts and whistles, then a long sigh as plops sounded. Hannah clamped her hand over her lips, the smell of fresh human shit so oddly welcoming. Just so normal. It was just so normal here except for the odd boss zombies slumping here and there.

"Sorry! I couldn't hold it anymore." The woman next to Hannah said, a cheerful grandmotherly voice. "When you gotta shit, you gotta shit."

"Absolutely," Hannah said, flushing her toilet, leaving her stall. She washed her hands, the soap in the dispenser a bright violent pink that smelled of roses. Cheap roses. Her reflection showed she did seem pale. Her face was her face—her little round chin, her snubby nose, the winged eyebrows she had always liked—but there was no giant scar from plunging through a barbed wire fence as three zombies tried... No giant scar. She was not starving or filthy. Her hair had somehow grown back and she had somehow added blond streaks to it. Her gray-blue eyes had been rimmed with brown, her lashes clumpy with mascara. Silver eyeshadow smeared on her lids. But she had never been good at applying makeup. More plops and sighs from the woman taking a monster afternoon shit. Sensible shoes, thick ankles, thick legs encased in dark hose. Hannah left her to it.

That very long hallway, with big offices and the break room and the main room full of worker bees... Bright overhead lights. Big windows that looked down on a city street. This was still Boise. She was still Hannah G. Gray. She looked at her left wrist. A faint scar ran from her wrist to her elbow, a jagged faint pink line. She remembered the blood pooling, the smell of hot crushed pennies. She did not remember this office or these people.

PART THREE: MISS GRAY AND MR. HARRISON

"Ahem. Miss Gray?" A low voice, of authority, banking and Wall Street matters. The low gritty voice of a walking corpse. *Zombies don't talk, damn it. They grunt and try to eat you. Everyone knows that. Everyone!*

The zombie in the bright canary suit. She faced him, having been caught staring out the big window. "Yes? Um. Sir?"

"Are you okay? Is that letter done? We don't have it yet and we're late getting the invitations out. We've had to deal with the PR for all that FF nonsense. Honestly, what do those people want? Such hysterical overreactions on their part all the time. Every little thing magnified a thousand times. Of course, that can be made to look very bad! We need to get back on track, Miss Gray."

She nodded. His smell ... ripe decay hidden by some powerful men's cologne. *Old Spice can't fix everything,* she thought. "I'm doing it now."

"Great. And did they tell you cheese and crackers tomorrow? Havarti." His eyes held red bulgy veins. "Jodi's bringing her potato salad, it's a last minute decision. She enjoys making things with eggs these days. Humor her, I say."

Hannah blinked, her mind just going blank for a long, long time at this random, weird spate of information and office politicking. *Fuck the potato salad, we're going in, boys!* Oh the strange things that ran through the brain tissues at times. "Okay. Fine. Havarti." She was not even sure that was a cheese. Was it?

"Can you come into my office, Miss Gray? I have

another matter I wish to discuss with you, if you have a moment." Canary zombie actually let his eyelid droop a bit. A wink. A wink! She clenched her hands. Alone with a zombie. But he was just one. She could kill him if she had to.

"Uh ... sure." Hannah followed the zombie into his big, square office, which had a large framed print of a ... yes, nuclear explosion that graced an entire wall by itself. *Bikini Atoll* read the caption. A gigantic black metal and oak desk, a Mac, a printer on a small table, and a nameplate that read Harrison P. Squack. Squack. *Was that a real name?* He closed the door and she spied three things to use as weapons. A letter opener, a glass sculpture of a naked baby—a cupid?—and the picture itself of that nuclear explosion. The frame could be broken and turned into a stabby. Glass shards could be jabbed into face or body. She had learned, she had learned, oh yes, to make weapons from thin air. Yep.

"Have you told Kevin? About us?" He spoke as if they were dear friends, more than friends. As if they knew each other. Really, really knew each other.

What had the giant zombie canary just said? "What do I tell Kevin, Harry? About what?"

"You know I hate being called Harry. Ah, baby. Sweetie! I know you're angry. I'm not good at this. I'm not a relationship sort. I know you said we could make it work... I'm working on that, okay? But you gotta break it off with Kevin. I'm old-fashioned. And he's trouble and no good for you. But you girls seem to like that type. I don't get it." Harrison sat on the edge of his desk, saying these absurd, soap opera words to her, in an office run by zombies. She had died and woken up in hell, for sure. *Just go along, Hannah, you fucking idiot, until you know what's what.* Her little voices had never betrayed her. She listened to them religiously.

"I am. Tonight. I didn't want to do it over the phone. "

"Really? You say that all the time. I don't want to think you're in the Fecto Fighters. I don't want to think that, Hannah." Harrison let out a giant sigh. His breath ... her eyes watered from it. Fecto Fighters? Was that a band or a guerilla group? "You okay? You seem freaked out or something. Are you freaked out by all this, by me, by this? I am too, baby." His fingers reached out to touch her and she went backwards. He went very still. "We're at the office. I can't play zombie and prisoner right now. Just save your panties. For later."

Holy angels and creeping Jesus... Zombie sex games? Her gorge rose. She had watched zombies shred their victims alive, that relentless zombie drive to eat, eat, eat; a crowd of zombies could consume someone in about ten minutes. She had watched them, from a window high up. She had watched that.

"Sorry. You just get me so hot, Harrison. I'm sorry." What did a zombie do with used panties? *Oh sick, gross! Oh no, no, no, mind, no!* But her mind supplied this super-thin freak zombie having fun with a pair of white granny panties. *Stop it, stop it, pull it together right now, Hannah!*

"Oh. It's okay. I'm hot, too, Hannah." And he kissed her. His tongue tapping and curling around her shrinking tongue, his skeletal arms about her, his body bones and death and carnage. He even squeezed her bottom and she moaned to keep this game going a bit; she had to stop herself from just screaming and screaming. Or beating him to death with his own ripped-off arm. "You're so understanding of us, Hannah. I knew you were a good egg. Us Fectos appreciate when one of you understands us so well."

Fectos. The zombie called himself a Fecto. "I'm a great

egg," she whispered, wanting to scour her mouth with acid and bleach and rip out her tongue and get it dry cleaned. "You Fectos aren't as bad as they all say."

Harrison stopped, he had been about to sit down. Black wiry dead hair. It would probably come out in clumps if grabbed... He stopped all movement, his muddy eyes coming to Hannah. Mud-colored. Not a real color — death took your eye color and turned it muddy. "Who says that, Hannah?"

Damn. "It's just a saying. Nobody says that. Like it's not as bad as it seems or the early bird gets the worm."

"You tell me if there's talk like that. It's bad for relations. We have to keep a positive outlook or we're toast. It falls apart. Dissent and rancor helps no one."

Worse than a zombie tongue mating? "Okay, sure. I haven't heard anything like that, not really."

"Well, if you do, baby, you tell me, okay?" A smile, the careful smile of a shark. His skin still had a freshness to it. He was a new zombie or ... or maybe science had discovered how to preserve the zombies a bit. Mm. Google. She had a computer at her desk. It had to be linked to the internet. They'd need the internet at work, at whatever this place was.

"I will. I'll tell Kevin tonight."

"Okay," Harrison met her eyes, blew her a kiss. Ugh, a bug! She made herself smile and then left his office, sickened, confused and amused. Her evil twin was involved in some rancid office romance with the GODDAMN BOSS? Jesus! The goddamn zombie boss.

Once back at her desk, she copied and pasted the vague words about a fundraiser for Christmas, changed that to Halloween, found the Winnemucca office address and the Boise one, and copied and pasted those to the right side of the letter. It seemed so weird and natural to be doing this.

Before the zombies, she had been a cashier at Target. This seemed much the same work, only she didn't wear a smock. She managed to find an email for Jodi Fraggle... Really? Fraggle? This had to be the same Jodi, right? She attached the letter to her email and sent it off, without giving a hoot if it was right or not.

Ah, now for the internet.

All the social media sites seemed ... gone. No Facebook, no Twitter, Snapchat or Tumblr, no Instagram or... There was Chathead and something called Twiddlebuns. Both promised a 'zombie-human unified experience'... What the hell? Hannah tried looking up news about zombies and got an instant scary-looking screen that warned her she was using punishable terms and the items she had entered were restricted access only. What the actual what...? Was she still even in America? No. No, hell was not in America, surely.

"Uh... Sunni?" Hannah stood by Sunni's desk as Sunni highlighted text in a thick stack of closely typed prose. Sunni held up a finger, highlighted a sentence in bright orange, and then put her highlighter down. The wrapped boxes had disappeared. No, they had gone to another desk where no one sat.

"Sorry, I have to start the whole page over if I lose my place. Yeah?" Bright brown too-friendly eyes. Sunni was after Kevin and evil twin Hannah hungered for zombie manflesh. Just ... no. No.

"What happens when you type the word zombie...?"

Sunni's mouth fell open, she actually put a finger to her lips. "Shh!"

"Why can't you type that word? I'm doing some research for a fundraiser. Remind me again." Hannah knew she was not being very clever but she also didn't want to attract the wrong kind of attention. Going to Jodi or the love machine in yellow was not an option. Maybe the happy shitting grandma. Maybe she'd know.

"It's offensive. It's outlawed, they outlawed it, it has such negative connotations. We all voted on it, you voted on it, years ago. Jesus! You might as well bring a flamethrower to work tomorrow. There was only one box to check but we all still voted, you know? Tradition!" Sunni took a candy bar from her desk drawer and, ate it in a few gulps. "You want one?"

"Yes. I do." Hannah took the chocolate bar and ate it, right there. She'd not had a candy bar in over a year. The taste of it. It took away that nasty kiss, it seemed to smooth the rough jagged edges of her brain as it tried to make sense of all this. Real chocolate. It wasn't old or grainy. Real chocolate. Zombies had a chocolate factory up and going? Zombies didn't eat chocolate. "Thanks, Sunni."

"Oh hey ... about Kevin. I did that for the ... you know, the FF," the peach-scented spy whispered that last part, as if it was supposed to make sense and ring all the right bells. She even winked, which Harry the Giant Zombie Canary had done. Winking, it seemed all the rage about these here parts.

"Sure, yeah. The ... yeah. Fectos, huh?" Hannah had no idea, yet again, of what this peach-smelling idiot babbled about. "I'm writing a pamphlet on them. For PR." Score, hit – yes, yes, yes. Hannah felt very clever and sly. "Jodi, you know. So... I can't look up the z word. What...what's the official title or whatever?" Surely anyone with any sense could see this was not the evil twin that actually did all this crap here in zombie office hell. But not dear Sunni!

"Infected Ones. Fectos. That you can look up. It should be a hoot. If I want a good laugh, I look up Fectos on their official website. I really am sorry about Kevin. It had to be done. Sorry we didn't tell you beforehand. Sorry it was so public. It throws them off to think we're fighting over that pipsqueak." Sunni looked around, snuck another plain chocolate bar from her desk drawer, tore it open, and then crammed it into her mouth. Hannah nodded, chocolate coating her throat. Hannah went back to her corner desk, at the very back of that giant office space and sat at her computer again. She opened her company email and there was a reply already from Jodi.

Not acceptable. Redo this.

Hannah closed it and instead, typed in Fectos into Google. At least Google still existed here. Fectos. Infected Ones. And then she smelled zombie aroma and heavy cologne. Canary zombie Harrison. She had not heard him slither to her desk. *You're dead, girl, you're dead,* she thought.

"Hannah, is this the best use of your time?"

"Nope. Anything else, sir?" Her mind helplessly supplied this super-thin zombie guy who sniffed row of underwear. Sniffing. Hundreds of pairs of underwear and he went along the hundreds of rows, sniffing. Her teeth clenched, her stomach clenched.

Their eyes met; her eyes wanted to find something else to stare at. His eyes dipped to her sweater puppies and back to her face. Oh shudder. "Jodi is very upset. Is it the potato salad decree?"

"Of course not. Cheese and crackers, whatever. It's the newsletter. I'll redo it. I didn't have any details, so I just did a generic one. I'm sorry. If I had the details, I could add the details, sir." She kept her tone very polite and professional but Harrison frowned. A letter opener, jammed in his crotch, might turn that frown upside down.

"You have the information, we sent it you. We talked

about it in the meeting just this morning, before Lana got a bit excited. It's the big Halloween Gala. The Monster's Romp. Ghostbird agreed to play for next to nothing, which is a deal. We got Ghostbird. That's big, Hannah. We expect to raise over a million dollars for charity causes, including those wandering about out in the Eatery. For the victims of that breach over in Oregon. We're raising money to build shelters. We're...! You know all this, Miss Gray. This is not the way." He lowered his voice, bent down closer, tapped at her computer screen as if showing her something. "This is not the way to get back at me for making you end it with Kevin. You're a very greedy girl, Miss Gray. Or you're dangerous. I'm not sure which yet." A tiny fissure in his cheek. Rot. A little rotting fissure in his cheek.

"Am I also being promoted like you promised?" Hannah threw out, wracking her brain for every bad soap opera plot she knew. Harrison reared back, that whiff of death and cologne congealing in her nostrils.

"We'll get married, you'll stay at home. I'll take care of you, you won't have to do anything but paint your toenails. Promotion to what? You're as high as you can go, Miss Gray. Everyone wants to work in the Bureau of Humans. Please don't turn into some disenchanted whiner, or someone who doesn't know their place in the scheme of things! Everything is nearly perfect, the balances work. Don't go messing with that, it's chaos and madness! It's unnatural to want more than what you're capable of. You want real freedom, baby, go wander the Eatery!" He breathed hard, that zombie breathing, that heavy rattling breath from lungs that should not be moving or squeezing or however lungs worked. *Are you full of worms and maggots, Harry? Are ya?* "Now get that letter done, correctly, please. If I have to come check on you again... Well."

"What will happen? What's the Eatery? Shelters? We build shelters here? We're a charity?"

For a moment, she thought his head would start spinning. Then, he smiled, that unpleasant splitting of zombie lips, the shine of spit on chompie teeth. "You know what we are here, Miss Gray. How you tease me. It's delicious. I can't resist you when you tease me so. I'll see you later tonight. If you haven't broken with Mr. Taggart, then you will be punished." The way he said punished was the way others said cheesecake.

Harrison went back to his office, nodding to this working gal or that one. Hannah considered all that, and made herself expunge that bit about zombie S and M games from her memory for all times. Except. there it was: the lumbering monster, her tied to a tree ... and the monster literally eating her and pinching her nipples as he did so. Gross. Some word far more profound than gross. *Like, ewww, super-gross! Abomination. Infection. Super-awful gross.* That chocolate bar sat very uneasily.

"Hey, are you two gonna announce anything yet?" A hand clapped Hannah's back a little too hard. A new woman, with sensible shoes. The happy grandma-voiced shitter? Lank gray hair, pinned back. Bright Nordic blue eyes, maliciously happy Nordic blue eyes. A square heavy face, three long white hairs sprouting underneath that weak chin. "You're so smart. Attaching to a Fecto like that. How do you do it? Doesn't he turn your stomach? They all keep teen sex slaves. They snack on puppies. How do you do it with a zombie? Aren't they, like, you know..." The grandma smiled after saying such not-grandmotherly things.

Danger. Hannah sensed that malice coursing at her. Lana? Was this the Lana that Sunni had mentioned? She saw not-Katherine peering at her, shaking her black head. "What are you talking about, Lana?"

"You know what I'm talking about, you sly minx," Lana said with a happy, grating little chuckle. Nailed it! This was Lana. "We all want out of here. You found a way out but man, what a price. I hear they can't, you know … because of their disease. There's nothing down there, it rots off first thing. They're like lepers."

PART FOUR: I'M A PEASANT

Oh man. Oh holy Jesus. Lana winked, then went back to her desk at the very front of the twenty or so desks, most of which did not have occupants. Halloween Gala. Fectos. The Eatery. Hannah sat back in her swirly, padded chair, staring at the picture of her and the poor, handsome Kevin. Phone. She must have a phone. Ah. Purse, in the third drawer. She yanked it out, a purple and blue number with a fringe. A small cheap bee pin. Why on earth would her evil twin go out in public with a purse like this? A flip phone that had half a battery left for a charge. She got to the contact list. Kevin. She dialed, then looked around to make sure no one had come to feel her up or mock her or see if she was writing fundraiser letters.

Someone answered on the second ring. "Hannah? Aren't you at work?" A rather squeaky male voice, like a cartoon mouse. Surely not. Pipsqueak, that Sunni had called Kevin. Ah!

"Kevin?"

"Yeah. You called me. Shit. Is he right there? Tell him we broke up! God, you're so slow, is this deliberate? Are you on your cell? This isn't the company cell?"

Intrigue. Oh my. Kevin did not talk like a boyfriend. He talked like a Batman villain. Or one of those fanatics who got people to murder entire housefuls of people for a cause of some sort. Like the right to make potato salad for a company potluck. "Is this Kevin? Are we running away to wander the Eatery?"

"What? Uh, no. We're heading toward Chile. This weekend. I've got it arranged. We'll be free of them."

Free of them. That sounded great. Except ... it seemed

everyone here had a job, money, security, food. The zombies seemed not hungry at all for human flesh, other than kinky sex games. Not so bad, really. Yes, that is bad, Hannah amended. *That's bad—yep, yep, yep.* "So I tell Harry everything is good?"

"Yeah. Why are you calling me from the office? You know Lana and Ophelia and the rest of them keep tabs and spy on all this. We suspect Sunni and Jodi have ties, don't trust her. Sunni, I mean. Don't tell Lana anything. In fact, just don't talk at all, to anyone there, except when necessary. You know what happened to Jenny and Orvi. That was ugly. Look, I'll be over tonight."

"Uh, no. Harrison said he was coming over. Probably with some lube."

Silence, then a slight laugh from Kevin's end. A shrill humorless blast of sound. A drill boring into her temple. "A sense of humor can really help at times, I agree. You call me after he's gone. All right? You let him ....whatever. He can't really penetrate you. He can't defile you. Just think of how free we'll be of them soon. When he's..."

"Jesus, all right. I get it. I'm a possession; this is the goddamn Fifties or something. Bye." She ended the call before she just yanked Kevin's teensy dick off and stuffed it up his ass. She had not lived—sort of lived—through a zombie infestation of the entire planet to put up with a Kevin or a Harrison or any of this shit. She stood up. *Be smart,* her little voice spoke up suddenly. *Zombies, they're almighty damn dangerous so sit down.* Hannah sat. Let Sunni have Kevin. Or Jodi. Lesbian zombie forbidden love? Whatever. They could all go to... Chile. Who ran away to Chile? She wasn't even sure where it was.

Jodi came out of her office and came into the general office space, making a beeline for Hannah. "I'll just do the letter myself. I'm very disappointed with you today,

Hannah." Jodi couldn't send another email? Or use a phone?

"Fine. I think that's best. I'd just mess it up, again. You write that fucking letter, Jodi."

Silence and the notion that all ears had swiveled to the back of the room.

"What did you say to me, Miss Gray?"

"Nothing. I said nothing at all, ma'am."

"You cursed at me."

"I don't recall that, ma'am," said Hannah with a big smile. If they were going to kill her in this version of whatever, she'd go down with a giant shit-eating grin and a letter opener buried in Jodi's soft eye meat. "Anything else?"

"No," Jodi said, in a very ominous obvious way. She returned to her office, stopping to speak to Sunni. Jodi would, no doubt, compose a You're Fired email. Hannah returned to searching Fectos, the Eatery and what had happened. She found nothing on any wars or infections or legions of zombies turning the world into a giant graveyard. There was just a wall of nothing. Any time she tried to investigate what came before the nice Fectos took over everything and made the world great again, there were just warning screens or blank screens that redirected her to shopping sites. Apparel by Kimmy, every time. She went to the certified Fectos site and saw PR pictures of carefully dressed zombies doing everyday normal stuff. A picnic. Opening presents around a Christmas tree. Dressed up as a nurse for a Halloween party. Singing on a stage wearing a ball gown. Zombies sang? Being the president—a woman zombie president. Of course. A woman had to die and come back from the dead to be elected president of the United States. Karen Jamwich. Fifty years ago . Such odd names, as if children had made them up. That was fifty years ago. What? That didn't fit with the zombie plague starting about five years ago or so. There had been two other female Fecto presidents, both looking like gray-faced church wives. The stiff wigs, the little choker of pearls, the thick shapeless suit that hid their figures. *Who was that English prime minister gal? Hatcher? Thatcher!* Those American lady zombie presidents all looked like Thatcher, with that same hate-you-motherfucking-peasants face.

I'm a peasant, thought Hannah.

All three Fecto female presidents had the same harsh, easy to offend air to them, even in still pictures. The videos ... geez. The careful crowds, the adoring chants. *The world is great again, the world is great again; we love you, we love you.* So staged-looking, so obvious. The humans love us now, was one of the slogans from the Early Days, as the site so carefully cited.

The Eatery also proved a dead end. Nothing. Just nothing except a list of restaurants. All local Boise, Merinampwell... Wait... Someone had shoved Meridian, Nampa and Caldwell into one word or ... or it had been reduced into one little town. She dared type in Idaho and looked for maps. A big ring that started above Merinampwell and went all the way to Winnemucca. Just a perfect circle with roads and towns and the Boise airport listed. Oh, and Mountain Home and the air force base. Beyond that circle, however, was just a black space and then another circle, from Salt Lake City over toward Denver; a circle that ended on the other side of Las Vegas. Just big circles of population and then splotches of black, as if the areas in the circles floated. The Boise-Winnemucca circle had a number: five.

The Salt Lake one had four. Whatever was west of Boise was probably six or seven. Portland-Seattle, probably seven. But she could not get the map to show that. It just kicked her back to Apparel by Kimmy, everything fifty percent off. She tried to look at the Salt Lake one; again, she found herself at Apparel by Kimmy and now everything seemed to be sixty percent off, for the next ten minutes. Hannah had never been good with computers and the one she sat at seemed to be alive and playing tricks on her. She tried the Eatery again and got directed to a mail-order steakhouse in McDermott, Nevada. The steak-order business promised life-like taste. Real meat taste, it promised. What the hell did that mean? Maybe it was like those hamburgers made out of beans or lentils that the vegetarians liked to pretend tasted like a real hamburger.

Hannah sat back, her fingers cramped. She had grown so used to being hungry and thirsty that watching the older woman at the desk two up from her drink casually from a water bottle mesmerized her for a bit. *Was the water clean? Had it been boiled? Was there any iodine or bleach? You're in hell, the food and water here are clean, Hannah! It's just the rest of it that's flooky and off.* The big clock that looked down on them all said it was four thirty-five. Sunni continued to highlight things in her stack of papers. She looked on automatic pilot. Lana talked on her small phone and then tapped something into her computer, nodding. Customer service? Complaints? Sex phone operator? Not-Katherine seemed determined to fill even more files with little numbers. Jodi and Harrison spoke in the outer hallway and they kept looking toward her. Great. She had made a real balls up here. *The Canary and Muslim Zombie Boss Lady thought her a naughty little secretary! Oh my!*

So. She was in some world where the zombies, called Fectos, ran everything. Humans were strictly low rent worker bees and made to do busy work. Zombies and humans got married. Ew. Fine, whatever. Boise and probably other cities were now like those walled castles or like Berlin at one time. Walls or barriers that kept out ... the monsters. Of course. The zombies did not want to join the Illuminati. Or whatever had happened. Hannah had read about the Illuminati when Target had been slow, once upon a very long time ago. A secret supergroup poised to take over the world any day now.

Except everyone knew about that super-secret evil supergroup. She had read articles on how it was the Illuminati that were spreading the weird, aggression-causing virus from their mansions in New Jersey. That the liberal elites had joined in with the Illuminati to take over the world and were using germ warfare to do so. And chemtrails. And vaccines. And all those drugs given to people with depression, when everyone knew depression didn't actually exist, it was just doctors trying to make money off you. The only way to fight all that was to live clean, save sex for marriage, end abortion for all time, and to get right with Jesus. *They can't infect you if you're armed with the truth!*

Which struck her as really funny near closing time on a Saturday night, when people came sneaking through to buy junk food and massagers. Those Jesus shouty types always seemed to get caught with their hand down an underage hooker's pants or caught padding an off-shore bank account with stolen funds, or both at the same time. Why anyone bought into that crap! Except they had. Hadn't it gotten so very awful before everything just fell apart and broken forever?

"A half hour, then we can go," said not-Katherine. Hannah looked up at her.

"What's your name? It's not Katherine?"

The woman pulled up the empty chair next to her, the same one Sunni had used. She smiled at Hannah, a fake smile. "Did you drop that Skeezie?"

"Uh ... yeah. Yep. I don't know anyone here. I killed myself and woke up in this weird office and got tongue-kissed by that canary zombie guy." Hannah said cheerfully, with the same fake smile plastered on her face. The pill rested in Hannah's pocket. She was not about to pop something like that, without knowing what it did. "Here. Have the rest back." The woman took the opaque little bag quickly, eyes going wide. She stuffed it down her front.

"Just keep that to yourself, Hannah. I'm Phil, Ophelia." Phil leaned very close, as if looking at something on Hannah's computer. "This entire place is bugged. Wired for sound." She jerked her head at the wall, nodded at Hannah. "Yes, that looks like a virus. You might need IT up here." Phil put a finger to her lips for a second or two, shifted her eyes to the wall, then back to Hannah. "We'll go in about half an hour. You want a Coke or anything?"

"Sure, I must have some change or..."

"Honey, they're free! We get free coffee, free pop, snacks. We're well taken care of here." Phil rose to her feet and trotted off. Hannah sat there, staring at the cream wall. Behind her was a big window. She turned and looked out. Everything looked so normal. If this was the New World Order, great. Free snacks? Snacks that were actually edible? Not crawling with germs and diseases and filth? Phil came back with a Coca Cola in the requisite glass bottle, ice cold, with a straw. And two sugar cookies. Bakery kind or from the store. "You get some caffeine and sugar in ya. It will help."

After a candy bar? Yep, probably. "Thanks. This is all free?"

"Are you trying to be funny? We're the government here, kind of. They take care of us, try to keep us happy. The Bureau of Human Affairs is a great place to work," Phil announced like something out of a really bad commercial. Hannah had already eaten the two cookies and had drained the Coke in about three giant sucks. She burped long and hard and Phil laughed, a real laugh. It did not quite taste like the Coca Cola she remembered. Close enough, though. Bubbles and teeth-rotting sweetness, that was all a working gal needed to make it to quitting time.

Hannah found she could leave with Phil. Jodi and Harrison just looked at her, then went into their offices. She hesitated, but Phil dragged her toward the elevators, where others waited to go downward. No zombies. Just humans. Mostly women, wearing overly sedate, unwed librarian type outfits. They murmured at her and Phil, and Hannah and Phil murmured back. Going home time. Miller time. Did they still make beer? Down, down, the elevator plunged—eight floors. It opened on a black marble-floored, very tasteful lobby, with two zombies standing at the door—big ones. The women straggled out, with hardly a look at the two guards in their dark purple uniforms, BH emblazoned on their chests. Bureau of Humans. Boise was still Boise. Phil led her to a small, cherry-red Chevy pickup. The sound of the doors unlocking. Where would they manufacture cars and such if most of the country had been blacked out?

"Okay. What is with you today?" Phil backed up, got them onto Myrtle and headed off into the heavy traffic. Except ... it seemed light and sporadic, as if people were pretending the traffic was heavy and not.... "What?"

The cross street had said Dog's Bark Parkway. Hannah could not remember, ever, a street or road in Boise with that name.

"The traffic seems light. Dog's Bark. Is that new?"

"It's not. The Skeezie will wear off. New? No. You really are out of it. Did you pop something else, Hannah? A Partygal? A Deaddick?"

Warning bells. *Trust no one, Hannah. Trust no one. Not even friendly-seeming sorts who had rampant bouts of actual paranoia.* "No, I'm okay. I'm fine." Another intersection—Myrtle and Happy Poppyseed. Good grief.

"What were you saying about kissing Harrison? I mean, we all know. But... We also know you can't really refuse them. Poor Lil, her mother should have scarred her or something, right? You can't refuse them, ever. That would be, gosh, suicidal. They get what they want and we get to keep on living, you know?" Phil fumbled in her purse, got out her phone, checked it, put it back. "He's not so bad. Nothing like Henry. Henry cornered me once, when he was here doing an inspection of our books. There was that party—you know the one. Where we had havarti that first time. Now we always have to have havarti. They like tradition. Harvarti is now tradition! They don't even eat the damn stuff! But they have to have it, oh yes, oh my! That party."

"I don't, actually. Skeezie fog, big time Skeezie fog."

"Ah," Phil dared take her eyes from the near empty road to frown a bit at Hannah before putting her eyeballs back where they needed to go. "It does make you go all foggy, doesn't it. Well ... that big party last year. I was getting the reports out, we print them out for some reason. Nothing else they want printed out. Okay, well, I was in that little back room. Henry came in, closed the door and ... did things to me. Until Jodi came in, looking for copier paper. She just calmly sent me on some errand. But every time he shows up here, she makes sure I'm elsewhere. I think her and Sunni are friends, if you get my drift." Phil rolled her eyes, winked over at Hannah, and then continued her tale of Zombie Party Tales. "I took three showers. I got drunk. What can you do? You can't report it. Everything the Fectos do is pretty much within the laws, after all. Laws are for humans only. Like Dandy would allow the cops to jail one of his own? Are you kidding? You can't fight them. Helen put a stapler through that one executive and she just ... went away to 'the Salt Lake office'. Ha ha, right? Lil got sent to Las Vegas on a transfer, like we don't know we get sent there to die. I don't want to go away, Hannah."

"I hear ya, Phil," Hannah said. "So what did he do? Have we talked about this and I forgot?" Did he chase you around and play zombie... Hey, had Harrison used the word zombie? Instead of Fecto?

"Come on, Han."

"Can it be any worse than not fighting them and watching them eat your friend? And then running and hiding and being so glad they ate Madison instead of you? That was her name. Madison. Madison Priegal. We grew up together, over in Caldwell. Her dad grew corn and wheat. He was a nice man." Hannah stared out the window, noting the billboards and advertising. Zombie-positive. Aggressively so, to her eyes.

"What are you talking about? You sound like you were out in the Eatery. Or like a Hollow. You've never been out of Boise that I know of. You were born over on Orchard and Happyway? Isn't that what you told everyone? Caldwell? Where is that? Madison? That's Sunni's real name."

"Skeezie fog! It's a gas, gas, gas." Hannah laughed and laughed, determined to zip her lip from now on. Surviving meant fitting in and adapting. She'd have a much better day at work tomorrow and of course, not run off to Chile, for the love of all the fucks ever given, with some cartoon mouse-voiced doofus. But being a sex pet of that Harrison thing. No thanks. That had to end. She could cite it was her, not him. She just couldn't handle all that gooey goodness. Something like that. Her memory played that last week's highlights. Running and hiding and starving. Watching Lyle get careless. Jack just disappearing and finding his boot full of blood and three toes. Seeing Jack without an arm and minus those three toes. That apartment she had found, with a door still able to close. That glass vase with the hobo clown, the blood pooling in her lap, running over her thighs.

"Whatever's made you crack a bit, Hannah. Just get over it. They might look tame and safe, they're not."

"I know. Thank you. We're good friends, right?"

Phil patted Hannah's arm. "I like to think so."

"What's the Eatery? Is that where the zombies..."

"Don't say zombies. Jesus! Say Fectos or Infected Ones. President Jamwich, years ago, outlawed that word. It's death to utter it."

"No shit? It's what they are. Isn't this America? Freedom of speech?"

PART FIVE: IT'S THEIR AMERICA

Phil turned off onto a narrow windy street, Julia Lane, that led to houses and apartment buildings behind tall fences. "It's their America now, not ours, that's how I think of it. I just live here, it's theirs."

"What? Whatever. I'll be all better tomorrow. I ... I think I have the flu."

"Maybe stay home tomorrow until you get it together," Phil said. She stopped before a big black metal gate, with three sets of tall apartment buildings waiting for Hannah to play find-the-apartment. "Call me tonight if you're calling in sick."

"Oh. Sure. Are you ... picking me up tomorrow?"

"Well, yeah. It's my month. Don't take any more Skeezies. Not until the weekend, anyway. That's when I take 'em." Phil rolled the window back up and pulled back onto the street, drove away. Hannah cast her eyes about but she knew nothing of this neighborhood. It didn't seem the same yet it seemed ... real. A 7-11 at the corner, a dry cleaner, a hobby store. Just the usual neighborhood stuff. She tried the gate: locked. A keypad waiting for five numbers. She had never been able to afford a fancy apartment behind a gate in her other life.

A little girl with a big pink and green backpack came bopping along, with her brown hair cut cruelly short and a cut beneath her left blue eye. She punched in some numbers and the gate clicked. Hannah went through as well and the little girl stopped. Hannah stopped.

"Hey. You live here?" The little girl sniffed long and deep.

A big belligerent kid voice. Nine years old. Fast and

lean, no zombie could run down this little roadrunner.

"I think so. What's the code? I forgot."

"Fuck you, twatmama," the little girl said and then flipped Hannah off. She ran off toward the third collection of buildings. Hannah checked her wallet. Idaho driver's license. *Really? They still had a DMV?* Her address: 1226 Montrose Way, Apt. 12. Okay! No weight, no height, no codes. She turned it over, just a line for her signature. Oh. A small sentence about if she was found driving outside of Region Five, she'd face official punishments.

Her apartment was in the first collection of apartments. Just concrete boxes stacked on concrete boxes, painted a dull fading yellow-gray. A jarring sameness, more like a prison compound than apartments where one could come and go freely. These concrete drab dwellings started at one and went up. She walked over to the second building. Apartments started there at twenty-five. Back to her building! Number twelve was on the bottom floor, near the back, across from what looked like the communal laundry room. Great. A man poured his clothes into a washer, wearing gray sweatpants and a stained white t-shirt. He had a cute beer belly, a small one ... imagine that. Someone able to sport a beer belly. The all-zombies diet had been a real boon to the human race in a way. No one gave a shit about wobbly thighs, muffin tops and beery bellies when the zombies swarmed. The man, who needed to shave, looked right at her, saluted lazily, and then took his empty plastic clothes basket with him as he sauntered out and around the corner, to apartment 7. Which was on the first floor. Two layers of apartments, stacked atop each other. She found a wad of keys in her purse — her fringy purse — and managed to find the one that opened her door. A rush of cat-shit air and then a cat; a big tortoiseshell with melting lime green eyes. This cat greeted her ecstatically. She very nearly booted it through the wall then stopped herself.

After closing the door and locking it, Hannah just stared. A small beige couch that had probably come with the tiny apartment. A small kitchen where dishes waited to be washed. A coffee pot, turned off, with half a pot of coffee still left in it. A framed print of a movie she'd never heard of—Corners of Sanctuary—starring someone named Bill Kilgore and Jessica Ulkatz. A man pictured from the back, head down. A woman with very long, light brown hair puddled at his feet, wearing a see-through nightgown. Vines wrapped about both figures, and painted in the distance was what looked like a small barn or a large storage unit. That movie had apparently won every award known to man and zombie kind. She then saw it atop a stack of DVDs, near a flat-screen television set, a smallish one. *A Fecto fooled by an evil Fecto Fighter and his journey to redemption.* What the actual fuck? Hannah laughed, let the DVD fall from her hand to the burnt orange carpet. The whole apartment seemed done in burnt orange carpet and beige furniture. The drapes were an industrial beige-gold, with a tired swirl design. She opened them and got to peer at the next building over, with a walkway bordered by overlong grass and yes, piles of dog poo. The cat twined about her ankles and she petted it, discovered it wore a collar. Pebbles.

"Pebbles?" The cat looked up at her, purred, leaped up on the couch, kneaded the yellow blanket, and then lay down, tail twitching. "Do you know what's going on, cat? I sure don't." Why did it seem there was someone else here? Stop getting wigged out, she told herself. When had 'wigged out' been part of everyday life? Reagan? Carter? Nixon? Her knowledge of presidents had about six or seven names in the knowledge box. Lincoln, Washington,

Nixon, Carter, Reagan. Someone watched her, she knew it. Eyes on her skin, like moist little touches from blood-wet fingers. She listened. Just her and that cat. She closed her eyes, listened. Just her and that cat.

Hannah peeked into the bedroom. Her evil twin had not made the bed or picked up her clothes or indeed, seemed to care about neatness at all. Lotion by the bedside, a glass of water, a bottle of aspirin. Generic Western Family aspirin. A laptop charging, plugged into her wall socket. The bathroom held a toilet—that worked, a sink—that worked, and a shower—that worked. Three red towels, two under the sink, one hanging on a bar. A red round sponge hung in the shower. The shampoo smelled like sea air, or so it claimed. A box of tampons, a box of pads. Bleach, Comet, Lysol, basic cleaning products. She had two perfumes, in squatty glass bottles behind the bathroom mirror, both of which she hated. Forsythia Dreams and Floral Fantasies. A small makeup bag; very sedate muted colors, nothing wild. Fine, she hated makeup. It was a pain in the ass. A bottle of Pepto— they still made that, hurrah! Cream for itching ... vaginal cream for itching. She put that back on the small shelf and then closed the mirror back up. A yellow toothbrush. Colgate. It was odd. A mixture of items she knew and items she did not.

A small closet in the hallway, where the litter box lived. Wow, that needed changing. A sack of cat food, stacks of canned cat food and a big bag of cat litter. Great, the cat was well seen to. A small vacuum cleaner, a mop and a small red plastic bucket, and a broom and picker upper. Great!

Someone peeking over her shoulder... She turned but nothing there.

"Stop it, evil twin," she called out and did not feel like

laughing at all.

Hannah took a long, long shower until the hot water just went away and she started shivering. She washed her hair three times, soaped her entire body with the Vanilla Hopes body wash. A thorough scrubbing of her teeth and tongue, with the vaguely minty toothpaste. Colgate, but it tasted more like floury mint paste than what she knew to be actual toothpaste. Hannah wandered to the bedroom, the cat bounding ahead of her, and found a bathrobe. It was way too big; had to be Kevin's or some other man or zombie's. She combed her hair, noting it was not coming out in big clumps because she had not been eating or because she had not been washing it. A pair of sweats, a sweatshirt that featured a daisy front and center. It was either unmarried cat lady office clothes or cutesy loungewear worn by unwed cat ladies.

Food. She needed food. Was there any in the apartment? "Pebbles, is there any food?" The cat food, if she had to. It could be eaten. Soften the hard kind with water or urine, then just gulp down the wet. It could be done. "Pebbles! Any human food?"

Pebbles did not know. Pebbles hooked the strap of a filmy blue bra and had a nice time arching and spitting and attacking it. Hannah stood in the kitchen, clean and wearing clean clothes for the first time in a year. That ghastly office ensemble did not count. She could leave her drapes open, her door open, and the zombies ... would still come in, only they would make her write fundraising letters and try to finger her private parts.

There were canned veggies, some canned pork and beans. A couple cans of ravioli. Dried noodles. Top Hat ramen noodles: beef, pork, vegetable medley. Two of each. Spaghetti sauce in a jar. Mushroom soup, condensed. Cream of chicken, condensed. Single gal food, from an era long gone but now apparently back again.

The fridge held a casserole. She scooped out some with her fingers and tasted it. Bland, like ham, potato, pea and mushroom soup. But real food that someone — she — had actually cooked. Weird, too-sweet ham. Was it Spam or some other fake ham crap? She truly did not give a shit in a shiny bucket if it was. The ham pieces had a weird, spongy texture. She spat one out into her hand. It wasn't ham — it was some vegetarian-like substitute. She popped it back into her mouth, so used to eating whatever she could choke down.

A knock on her door. *Tap tap*, silence, *tap tap tap*. Code? Someone with OCD? Just somebody knocking?? She froze, then grabbed up a butcher knife. A big one. The only one in the drawer. Her evil twin only had one knife? She crept to the door, listened. What was she doing? That life was over. "Yeah? Hello?"

"It's me, Kev. We changed the code, remember? Let me in."

Squeaky mouse boy! Code, yep. She lived in a world where people knocked in codes. "Sure, just a minute." She unlocked the door. Kevin stood there in all his glory, looking like an escapee from some boy band. A really bad boy band. His thick chestnut hair fell just so over his artistic brow. He had REALLY SUFFERED. Kevin bent, kissed her — a peck on her cheek — then walked past her and took a seat on her couch. Pebbles at once found Kevin and came to greet him.

"Pebbles, nice kitty," this squeaky man said, petting Pebbles. Kevin looked at her with big sad dark green eyes. He had that movie star boyfriend look down pat. Wow. "Hannah, Sunni said you had a bad day at work. I have to treat her with kid gloves after what you told us about her and Jodi. Did you screw us over?"

"Why are you talking to Sunni about me? Yeah, her and Jodi seem close. Maybe they're friends. Maybe zombies need friends. I don't know. I don't know anything right now."

"Sunni's one of us. Or she pretends to be, but you can't trust anyone right now. They're winning with their nice zombie propaganda bullshit! Which you help write and distribute. Ah, Hannah. What happened? Did they turn you against Sunni and me? Sunni is still part of this, until she's not. I know how that sounds but you have to take chances, you have to. That damn Phil. I told you not to take rides from her. Did she notice the bee pin? I told you not to put it on your purse. 'Oh it's pretty', you said. You know they know what that bee is a symbol of! GOD DAMN IT." Kevin fluffed his chestnut hair, let his moist green eyes fill with righteous indignation for stupid, silly, vain Hannah. She clenched her hands into fists, over and over. "I know she probably feeds you Skeezies and then goes to town on ya, but fuck! God damn it, stop thinking with your snatch! Stop thinking this is just some fun game. This is real life, Hannah. People will die because of your mistakes and your careless bullshit. God damn it, Hannah!" Kevin tossed that head of chestnut hair, put his lips into snarl position. She hated him. Her hate came that quick. Boom, insta-hate. This was her boyfriend?

"Phil? She's nice, she drives me around. You leave Phil alone. God, you're an asshole." Hannah said, noting Kevin had a weak chin, noting that she thanked God for giving Kevin that weak chin. "Just get the fuck out."

"Phil?? She's working for them! How dare you talk to me like that? After everything?? Are you high right now?" He squeaked at her indignantly. "Did she try and slip you another Skeezie? A Deaddick? You'd swallow anything someone gave you, you're so well trained to swallow, ain't ya? God knows what's actually in them! God, you're so stupid. Ajeet was wrong to trust you. Garcia says to make you disappear. Whip saw you..."

"I also work for zombies, mister. I'm a happy little worker for zombies!" *Ajeet? Whip? Oh, this Kevin needed to go.* She itched to plant an axe in his head. That was her instinct right now: plant axe in Kevin's head. "Yeah, I've had seven Skeezers today, they're awesome. My boss is the only dead dick I've had to endure so far today. What job do you do? Do you have a job?" Hannah put her knife down, let him see her put that knife down. His shaggy eyebrows went up and down, up and down. "Do you want that movie poster on the wall? And the movie? And possibly the cat?" Pebbles purred and kneaded at the couch, doing that kneading the bread trick they all did.

"Harrison gave those to you, they're from the actual premier or something. You can't get rid of them now, what's the matter with you? Don't get cold feet on me now! It's all about to come together. I can forgive you. You're weak. We all know that, you're weak, weak, weak! But you're useful. Look—"

Hannah lost whatever control she had. She'd had enough of this asshammer. This was not a zombie. She did not have to be careful.

"Fuck off, Kevin or whatever your name is. Just get out of here. I've known you five seconds and I already hate you. You high-voiced boy band reject! Go. Get out." Hannah pointed at her door and Kevin just sat there, looking astonished. "Get along, asshammer!"

"You've known me how long? Are you trying out Hollow now for a new personality? It makes your ass look fat, honey." He stood, came right toward her and she backed up. He stopped. She took another step, hit her kitchen wall. "Shit. Did something happen with Harrison today? Or Jodi? Did they threaten you? We can protect you, Hannah. I'll get you to Chile and..."

"GET OUT OF MY FUCKING HOUSE," she roared and tossed a saucepan at him; it had been sitting on her stove, full of water. Maybe her evil other had made tea last night. Kevin got beaned. He had not been expecting her to throw things at him. The water splashed all over his nice dark gray button-down shirt and made it look like he had peed his pants. "Get the fuck out, mister. I'm gonna report you to Jodi and Harrison. I'm gonna tell them you said zombie! That you're the head of some group trying to take them down! Get out of my house! Fuck Chile! Who the fuck runs away to Chile?"

Kevin wet his lips, his tongue pink, repulsive and very short. A tiny little mini-tongue. "You're one of them. I knew it." Veins bulged in his temples, his teeth grinding, his hands curving into loose fists. He had a cut across the back of his left hand. Hannah took a step toward him, expecting him to go backwards, to head for the door, to call her names and go. Squeaky-voiced pretty boys were no threat to her.

"Sure, I'm one of them. You are so busted. Bye, Kevin! They know everything! They are so coming to get you. I'm a Hollow! I told them everything, Kevvie baby! EVERY LAST MOTHERFUCKING DETAIL, YOU TWATMAMA."

Kevin punched her. Just let her have it. She felt her nose break, and surely he had cracked her jaw a bit, too. Hannah slid to the floor, blood pouring from her nose. She laughed and when he tried to kick her, she grabbed his leg and bit him, smearing blood and snot and spit all over that slick trouser leg.

"You goddamn bitch. I knew we shouldn't have included you... Fucking kill you, you bitch. You're not going to ruin everything because some Fecto asshole finger-banged you and you liked it. You're some greedy shallow gold-digging whorebitch! You're the twatmama, not me!" Oh yes, her death had come and it was called Kevin. His hands went for her throat, his hands sought to crush her life away.

PART SIX: CLEAN UP

Hannah got to the butcher knife and buried it into Kevin's shoulder. She took up that useful saucepan and walloped him a good one. That real life of hers, where she had been fighting to stay alive near every day, came back to her now. *It was win or die, baby. Win or die.* Kevin screamed and roared. She sensed he was not used to fighting. He might have some muscle and height on her, but he was not a fighter of any kind. She gripped the handle of that butcher knife and yanked it free, causing him to yodel like a hound dog, blood splurting from his wound. She unzipped his guts, as she had learned to do on actual zombies. Slice open from belly to throat, a quick hard slice upward. Boom, guts everywhere and the zombie distracted. Except Kevin was not a zombie. He went down, screeching, trying to stuff his insides back inside himself.

"Hannah... Why... Why..." he moaned over and over. "Shoulda killed you... Shoulda killed you when..."

"Shut up," she finished him off, a quick throat-slit and he gargled blood for a bit, then went still. She breathed through her mouth, her face feeling numb yet tender and swollen, her nose clearly broken. Hot crushed pennies in the air now. How to clean this up and hide it? Her eyes darted about, then went to her purse. Zombies ate dead bodies. She scrolled through her numbers. Yes. Harrison. She dialed it and he answered, sounding stiff and professional. "Sorry to call you, sir," Hannah said, in case others were listening. "Is it safe to talk?" Her gaze went to the dead Kevin, to the mess and blood, to busted stuff laying all over. She had not even noticed things breaking during that fight. Plates, cups, cutlery.

"No, actually, it's not. Are you getting a cold? Can I call you back in about ten minutes? I'm in a meeting."

"Yes, sir. Thank you. Ten minutes. It's about the fundraising letter I botched." She felt truly inspired for tossing that out. Truly inspired!

"All right. No problem," Harrison said carefully and then the call ended. She sat on her couch, head hanging, and her blood flowing all over that burnt orange carpet. Had the neighbors heard all that? Ten minutes went by, then fifteen, then twenty. A half an hour. She applied a wet cloth to her face; oh, that felt good. Pebbles cuddled up to her for a bit, then went off for some cat fun elsewhere. Her phone rang. Harrison. Hannah answered.

"What are you doing, calling me so early? Are you okay?"

"I'm sorry. I really am. But… I just killed Kevin and I don't know what to do now. I think he broke my nose."

"You ... you what? You're what?"

Hannah recited how Kevin had come over, they'd had a bit of a tiff, and now he was dead on her kitchen floor. "Can you come over and eat him or something? Maybe bring Jodi and some of the other zo... Fectos?"

"Um, Hannah... Is Kevin really dead in your kitchen?" How hungry he sounded. Hungry was good! "Kevin Taggart is dead in your kitchen. My goodness. Score one for the good guys. No, I am not including that social climbing brain-gobbler in this. She's after my ass, Hannah. Don't ever think she's your friend and don't ever tell her anything that can be used against me. She'll be transferred to New Boston, she can play her social climber games there. I've spoken to Henry about this... Never mind. Now… Is Kevin really dead? In your kitchen?"

"Yes. I gutted him during our fight and then slit his

throat. He punched me. He started it. Well, I started it, but I just tossed a pan at him. He punched me. My nose is broken." *Score one for the good guys? Really? What side was her evil twin working? How many sides were there to work? There were plots, counter-plots and then counter-plots to the original plots. Who could keep all that straight or even want to?*

"He broke your nose?? I'm sorry, dear." A sigh from Harrison's end. He sounded as if he actually cared about her. A zombie with feelings. Other than 'chase, chase, rip-off flesh bits, munch, munch; oh look, it's still alive, time to eat some more of it' hunger, of course. "I'll be over in a bit. Don't do anything else. Don't let anyone else in. This will be all right. Daddy will take care of everything."

"I hope so," Hannah said dubiously. Chills at him referencing himself as 'Daddy'. Men who said things like that usually had torture dungeons full of neighborhood children. Or secret rooms full of tied-up naked female captives. *Wait now for daddy to come clean up her mess!* Maybe it would be better to call him back and just tell him to shove it, too. I mean, how would she pay such a favor back? But where would she stash a dead body? How many other apartment dwellers would watch her drag dead Kevin out to the trash and let her get away with it?

She had some of that bland casserole while she waited for Harrison. Pebbles sat by her as Hannah ate the cold casserole, from a plastic plate, with a tin spoon. No movement from Kevin so he really was dead, or playing possum. Hard to play possum with a slit throat and a slit belly. The smell of death, oozing blood, intestine contents, bladder and sphincter relaxing, letting go. No breath, no pulse, no life. Touching dead Kevin neither sickened nor saddened her; it was rather odd. She felt nothing much beyond a wish that the mess of him was already gone. She changed her clothes, and put her bloodied, torn ones into the hamper she'd found. Her wardrobe seemed dominated by browns, beiges, neutral tones and navy blue. Office clothes. Surely she should feel something for the man she had killed. Some remorse or agony or twinge. Her face hurt, and her soul lay dead and still within her.

Someone knocked and she stood by her door, heart beating a bit fast. "Harrison?"

"Yes. Open up."

Not by the hair of my chinny chin chin. "Why?"

"Why? You called me to clean this up, kiddo. Let's get it cleaned up," Harrison replied. She saw no fault in that logic, yet her senses tingled and buzzed. She was supposed to trust a zombie for help? *Trust a zombie not to utterly... ? Not go nuts and eat her seven ways of Sunday? This new reality held hidden pitfalls!* She wanted to laugh, she wanted to kill Harrison too, and just ... go off on her own. Let someone else take care of that damn cat, too. See what he does first, then decide, she told herself. That self actually snarled and frothed a bit.

The same canary yellow suit, the same smell of death under all that cologne. He went at once to stand over the dead Kevin, even nudged the body with his expensive loafered foot. Drool, was that drool on ole Harry's face? Yes. Yes, it was. "This is just a PR nightmare now, Hannah." Harrison said, turning toward her. "He's part of the Fecto Fighters, he's known to be one of them. He can't just turn up dead and partially eaten. What were you thinking? Huh. Your nose is broken. Look at that." His gray finger brushed over her cheek and she flinched back, then made a pain face.

"Ouch. It hurts. Look ... uh..." She nearly confessed she was new here and didn't know all the rules yet, or the players. Nope! "He hit me. I ... overreacted. But hey, we're broken up now. There's that, at least."

"It's okay, honey. Daddy's got this. It's okay. I'll call Jersey and Larry. We'll get this taken care of. Make it look like a suicide. Your kind gives in to despair so easily, after all. We'll toss him out a high window — splat. Splat goes the Kevin. We can't show that, but we can sure as hell say that's what happened over and over and over. Allow no other explanations, go after those who say he got killed for being a Fecto Fighter. You might have helped a lot more than you know, my dear sweetie." Harrison could not stop watching that blood, Kevin's pink coiled guts, and touching his long dry tongue to his chapped lips. Hannah tried not to watch Harrison stare at Kevin's dead body the way people used to stare at the Thanksgiving turkey. "I'll get the police to sign off on a suicide. Suicides are common among your kind. Dandy won't want the Fecto Fighters given any sympathy or power that martyrs can bring. His pretty wife can give a news conference about it. Truffie's very good at public speeches. Well, she used to be. She's gone a bit flop-headed, especially after that whole scandal. Poor Dandy." Harrison sounded more like he rather enjoyed whatever had happened to Dandy and his wife. Enjoyed it immensely. With a side of puppy brains.

"Why do you think we humans kill ourselves so often?" Hannah threw out there and Harrison, already dialing someone, gave her a look from his muddy eyes. A look that said to can it. A look that said Daddy would spank her if she kept being a smart mouth. She canned it. *Zombies were not human? They think they're better than humans*, she supplied to herself. And wanted to laugh. Hannah listened as he said cryptic things to unseen other zombies. She waited on her own couch as two hulking zombie flunkies came in, with a tool box and some industrial garbage bags, and cleaned up Kevin's remains. Daddy had delivered! They sawed Kevin into pieces. How could someone saw themselves into pieces if they'd committed suicide? That would have to be some wild, 'lie to everyone' press conference. *Are you truly that stupid, Hannah? Yes, yes, I am at times*, Hannah told that dry little voice.

Harrison led her to her own bedroom and made her remain there, behind a closed door, as the two worked in the kitchen. Hearing them work somehow seemed far worse than seeing them work. The crackle of stretchy garbage bags, the scrape of saw blade against bone, their low voices as if they were discussing the weather. Her and Pebbles waited for that mess to go away, that PR nightmare. Harrison remained out there, no doubt sampling Kevin. Taking gulps of Kevin's cooling flesh. Sucking Kevin's brains through Kevin's nostrils or something high end and elegant. They hardly talked at all, those zombies, and this seemed rather like a replay of her hiding in an apartment as zombies wandered nearby. She picked up her bedroom while she waited. Folded clothes, put them in her small cheap dresser, adjusted the boxes and bags on the top shelf of the tiny closet, lined up her shoes. Made the bed, retrieved underwear from beneath it and put it in the hamper. Looked at a photograph in a small black frame. There she was, yet that was not her. Her mother, yet not her mother, wearing a dress. Her real mother had never ever worn a dress. A man that looked like Hannah's long-gone daddy, who had actually gone out for milk and never come back. But yet, there he was, standing by Hannah's mom in that knee-length dress, smiling. In a tie. Like this had been snapped right after church. Hannah noted she looked about eight or nine in this strange, troubling picture. The house behind them did not look familiar, either. It had a porch with a wind chime made of old spoons. A big elm tree, and a giant cottonwood that had branches stretching over the peaked roof, ready to break off and crush it. A screen door. Two fragile steps leading down to the overgrown lawn. *Mow that, daddy!* This isn't my home, why is this here? Hannah put the framed picture on its face, hiding that bland, tame snap from a time and era she had absolutely no memory of; it didn't cling to any of the farthest corners of her brain. Her brain actually shuddered trying to place that picture, that house, that wind chime. Because that image would never show up, no matter how Hannah searched for it in the garbage cans of her own rememberings. Not even a faint misty outline of that house, those people and that moment.

"Hannah?" Harrison came right into her now-clean bedroom, eyes going a bit wide at how much nicer it looked when it was not a pigsty. "They're going to have to come back and clean."

"Okay. Great. Thank you."

"Uh huh." He came in, closed her bedroom door, and she hoped he hadn't turned all lusty all of a sudden. "This is a big deal but it's handled, okay? You need that nose splinted. I'll go get Dixie. He's been a good friend to us."

"Dixie, sure."

"I'd kiss you but you look like death warmed over," he said quietly, with a slight smile. "I expected hysterics from you, frankly. You've surprised me, dear. And you gutted that asshole like a fish and then bled him like a hog. Where, um, did you learn to do such things, Hannah?"

She gave a slight smile, then shrugged a little. "Oh, the streets. The mean streets of Boise."

"Good for you. I'm... I'm proud of you, Hannah. You're ... a good egg."

Her eyes met his. "I'm just trying to live, Harrison. And

not die. He tried to kill me. Was I supposed to let him?"

"No, of course not." He returned and then went, she assumed, to fetch Dixie. Hannah looked at the blood all over her kitchen floor. At the mess still left from dead Kevin. *I've made a deal with some real devils today,* she thought.

She sat on the beige couch, then put the Corners of Sanctuary DVD into the GE DVD player and turned on the television, also a GE model. Previews. For movies that looked stuffed full of zombie actors being menaced by humans. Curse of the She-Human looked interesting. Clowns and Rainbows did not. A slick documentary on Infected Ones … Year One Struggles, or some such crap. Then, a plea for funds to help the Eatery Victims of Philadillia. Yep, Philladillia, not Philadelphia. She checked the date of the DVD. It had been made about four years ago, if this was the current year. There were blurry pictures of actual zombies and what looked like a garbage dump. So the Eatery must be … everywhere the civilized zombies were not in charge. Then, the prompts for the movie itself. She hit the play button on the remote control and the movie opened, with no FBI warning. Nobody cared anymore if people were pirating movies?

Pebbles settled in beside her, purring. What a happy cat. Fog filled the screen. A dark figure walked in that fog. A low, husky voice told her that sometimes following the heart led to losing your head. The figure walking in the fog, she suddenly noticed, had no actual head.

"Fuck me," Hannah whispered. "How can you be talking if you have no head?"

Apparently, no one at the studios responsible for this film had considered that. She listened as that mournful male voice mourned love and all its pratfalls. Pratfalls. Even as that headless body stumbled about in an all-fog world. She stuffed her fist against her lips to stop from laughing, then remembered she didn't have to be quiet anymore. Laughter rang from her throat. Pebbles started up, then settled back down. How wonderful to make noise. How wonderful to sit on a couch watching an obviously bad movie, taking itself so very seriously, with the purr of an affectionate cat, with food in the cupboards, with drinking water nearby and a bathroom and a shower. With work to go to in the morning and bosses to deal with... Zombie bosses, but still. Killing Kevin seemed some goofy cartoonish dream; she dreamed all of this right now, and there were no consequences. Her face hurt, her nose slewed sideways for now. That damn Kevin had really cleaned her clock. And then she had cleaned his.

Harrison came right in, followed by a small actual man with a giant walrus-like silky gray mustache, silky brown eyes, and a medical bag. Hannah put the laughably bad movie on pause, just as Our Hero was about to meet Typical Woman Betrayer, at a meeting for Fecto-human relations or...?

"Ah, look at you, Miss Hannah!" Dixie had a gigantic, probably fake, Southern accent. "I got her, Mr. Squack. If you need to scurry off and be important." Oh my, that Dixie, what a card. Or he and Harrison were an item? Was being gay a big deal these days or not?

"Actually, I do have a few things to do but I'll be back to check on things later, Hannah. Larry and Jersey will be back to finish cleaning. Don't talk to them, either of you. Is that clear?" He gave them both a big politician's grin and they both smiled back, the smiles of slaves to their temperamental master.

"Got it. Am I allowed to ask what happened here?" Dixie sent his own fake as hell smile back at Harrison, who had taken a cell out to tap and beep and boop on it.

Those muddy eyes did not lift. Harrison had a smear of blood on his lower lip. *How did ole Kevvie taste there, Harry?*

"Sure. Just don't tell. I'll bring your payment when I come back in a few hours."

"You're too, too kind," purred Dixie, who stood maybe five foot one and had the body of a rounded puppy. Harrison smiled, a real one, and then left. Hannah turned to Dixie, who was already rooting about in his medical bag. "What the fuck, girlfriend? Who did this to your nose? Is it... You know? He slaughter a toddler in your kitchen? Again?" Same Southern accent, not as syrupy.

Wait. What? Never mind.

"We're friends, right?"

Dixie stuck a syringe into a small bottle of clear liquid. "Baby doll, of course we are. You tell daddy what happened."

"Can you not talk like a ... well, you? Are you a doctor?" Hannah eyed that syringe full of poison or magic Jesus pee, then stood. *Did the men and zombies here all call themselves Daddy? Gross.* Pebbles was heard scratching in the litter box. Dixie pulled back, clearly shocked. He had a round face and very pretty skin.

"I'm a vet, same thing. Now sit your fanny back down and let's see to that nose. You trying out a new tough girl routine?"

"You're a vet? What's in that needle?" Hannah moved away further.

"A mild pain killer and numbing agent, dear. So I can reset your nose. So why is there blood all over your dirty kitchen? What naughty thing happened here?" Dixie tapped that syringe. Waited for her to just comply.

"Oh, I killed Kevin. After he broke my nose. How's that for my new tough girl routine? What are Skeezers? Skeezies?"

Dixie patted the couch. She sensed no real harm coming from this little odd man. She sat and made a face as he tried to stick that needle in her cheek.

"Why did you kill Kevin? Are you taking his place? This place ain't bugged, we checked. Are you the new Humpalong?"

"What? What now? I... Stop trying to poison me! God damn it!" She simply shoved her nose back into place, letting out a cry but it seemed easier to breathe now. She spit out a mouthful of snot and blood onto the carpet as Dixie stared at her, eyes going as round as brown moons.

"What crawled up your back alley, Hannah? If you had orders to take out Kevin, great. Getting the Munchos to clean it up for you, well done. I'm on your side. Is this a test of my loyalties?" Dixie showed her the little empty bottle. "Cocospirin. Coke and aspirin, basically, for those who are not vets. Now dial it back a smidge."

PART SEVEN: WHAT'S WRONG WITH ALL OF YOU?

"That's... That sounds made up. I'm... I'm out of the ... group. Okay? I just wanna go to work and eat real food and..."

Dixie fell back against the couch back and stared up at the fake wood ceiling. At the light fixture, with a round plastic cover. "They got to you. They got to you, didn't they? Convinced you they see all, know all. It's bullshit, girlfriend. It's bullshit. I bet they even told you Chile's not real. It is! I know how tempting that Harrison is—he's got money and power and he's probably stuffing your twat with gold and good dildos. They lie. It's all they do; they lie about everything."

"Holy shit, can you not... That's so gross. And wrong. Zombies eat people, they don't... They don't want to screw 'em." Hannah spat another mouthful of phlegm, snot and blood onto the carpet. "What's wrong with everyone here? Is this hell? What's wrong with all of you?"

"Hannah." Dixie dug through his bag of magic and herbs and pet cough drops, came back up with a small prescription bottle. He opened this, and yes, shook two black pills into his palm. "You take these and you go away. And you wake up and you get that little head of yours screwed back on tight, or a whole lot of people are gonna die. They're just gonna toss us out into the Eatery, on the Oregon side, on the bad side of the Snake... We can't get back across it, there's just no way. Whatever he's been stuffing you with, you gotta realize, honey, he's still a Muncho and you're nothing to him. How many of those office girls does he have on the side? And his little pet slave at home? Golly! You think you're in love..."

"What are you talking about?? I am not in love with a zombie. What's the Eatery? What is it? I..." She went silent. *No, stop... Figure out what's going on here before mouthing off like an idiot.* She stared at her bare feet. She was clean. There was hot water for a shower. There was enough water to shower, flush the toilet, make some noodles, fill a glass. Clean water. "I'm just fucking with ya, Dixie. Kevin had to go, obviously. He was bad for us. Too visible. You passed the test, you're a loyal little shit. I like ya, Dix."

Dixie continued to hold out those two black pills. "You taking notes from that movie you're watching there, girlfriend? That's how Aurora acted. The Munchos thinks we're all like that. That we're all Auroras."

"Maybe I'm turning over some new leaves. Thanks, I'll take them when it's safe. Harrison is coming back." She now had three of these things. Hannah got up, put the two pills in her makeup bag, and then came back out after staring at her truly scary appearance. She had two black eyes and a big swollen schnoz. She had blood dried on her skin, smeared across her cheek. "Thank you for helping me. I'll tell everyone what a good egg you are."

"A what? I'm a what?? I... I was just joking about ... all I said. I was just joking, too. I gotta go. I was, uh, just testing you for loyalty, yeah, that's it." Dixie got up as if his ass had been lit on fire. He grabbed up his bag. "Hey. Uh. Those are just, uh, vitamins. I can take 'em back."

"What's the matter? I like your mustache."

"Nothing! Just don't tell anyone, um, important, I left you some harmless vitamins." Dixie had the door already opened. He bounced off, the door slamming behind his round puppy body. Hannah went over what she had said.

That egg comment. Good egg. Okay!

Off she went, chasing down Dixie, who trotted toward the third set of apartment buildings, in tears. She saw tears on his round cheeks.

"No! No, I won't go to the Eatery! I will not go to Salt Lake!"

"Dixie!! Dixie! Jesus. I'm not telling anyone about anything you said or did, okay? You're safe." She noted people watching this, then carefully ducking behind their ugly drapes. "I slipped. That egg comment, right? I slipped. I forget... I'm around them all day. The Munchos. I won't call you that again."

Those wet silky brown eyes regarded her warily. "I'm wound tight as a fiddle. I thought I knew you, Hannah. That's all. You seem like a whole new person right now and it's spooking the ever-livin' shit outta me." That Southern accent slipped a bit. *Why fake an accent like that in Idaho? Or whatever this circle was called. Boisia? Boiseland?* "Everyone hated Kevin but he was useful. He had contacts in New Boston. Oh poo on my houseplants, was he a SPY? Was he working with the Munchos? Why would Maureena have you take him out? You're not one of their trained squad! It's like everything's all wrong, nothing makes sense. I'm not a good egg, Hannah. I'm not one of their damn eggs."

She shrugged, already so tired of all this. This was almost more tiring than constantly running from zombies. "No, you're a bad egg, that's clear. Kevin's dead and we can all calm down. Just let the Munchies run shit—so what? We got food and shelter. What else, really, is there to care about?" *Being free to starve and fight them? No thanks! Been there, done that!* Hannah hated politics and she had somehow been dropped into a wasps' nest full of corruption, zombie power trips and revolutionaries. This is hell, after all, she concluded to herself.

Dixie stepped closer to her, clutching his medical bag. "You mean besides freedom and not being their slaves and having real lives? Oh nothing much, girlfriend." He gave her a glare full of hate and condemnation, then left her, his head up, his fat little bottom swinging as he stomped off. She went back to her apartment, and there were the two cleaning zombies, scrubbing slowly at her floor. Their eyes came to her and she nearly fled. These two did not even try to hide how hungry they were or that they wanted to sink their remaining teeth into her flesh. Carefully, she sat, let them finish, the smell of powerful bleach assaulting her nostrils. Pebbles came out of her bedroom, and then went back in, hissing. The two finished, took their buckets of cleaning supplies and rags with them, closing her door, giving her two tight nods that she barely managed to return. Alone. She was alone.

Hannah emptied that cat box and refilled it, after finding garbage bags beneath her kitchen sink. Where did the garbage go? Did she just throw it out with the other mountains of garbage that had piled up? In that other life? And she was starving. She wanted a cheeseburger, she wanted lasagna, she wanted roast beef and toast and popcorn, and a big pan of macaroni and cheese. Made with canned milk and Velveeta. She wanted chocolate cake. She wanted donuts, and celery sticks and raw carrots yanked from a garden. She wanted poutine, whatever that was. She wanted dumplings! She wanted an Easter ham and a Christmas turkey. Her stomach gave a giant growl. Oh, to be able to answer that with actual food, food, food. She'd put up with Hitler crossed with Darth Vader for a damn bologna sandwich and a glass of cold milk.

Get rid of the garbage and then stuff her face. That 7-

11 — she could surely find something satisfying and very expensive there. A tuna sandwich for four or five dollars. A wildly overpriced tiny bag of Cheetos. What money did they use here in hell? She didn't know her pin number for her ATM card, if they even had them here.

Wells Fargo Bank Americana. Whatever. A debit card with the Visa logo. Her name. Hannah G. Gray. Five numbers: 78560. She turned it over, there was her signature, a big loopy one. Information about the bank, which Region Five used but it was also good in Region 4. Great. If she got over to Salt Lake, she could withdraw money. Super. Where would she have her pin number info? Find that later or just go to the bank, when or if she found a bank to go to. People lost their pins or forgot them all the time.

There was a giant garbage bin near the front gates. She toted her bag of kitty shit and kitty pee out to it and then heard moaning from the other side of the big brick wall. The hair on the back of her neck rose. And then she saw it; a zombie, in tattered clothes, standing at the big metal gates, pawing at them, then catching sight of her. One eye glared, the other dangled down the ruined cheek. He had a chunk of his skull missing. "Pretty girl," he whispered at her. His tongue came out, waggled slowly back and forth across his split, desert-dry lips. "Pretty girl."

He wore what remained of a fancy suit. She could not move. No. No, not here, where it was safe. No. Weapon. Get a weapon. Hannah reached for a small rock. Once in her fist, it could bash in a soft rotting skull. Then, the slow, lazy splash of police lights. A voice that spoke through a speaker, a female voice. Comforting authority. "This is the Boise Police Department. Please go back inside. Do not engage with the Fecto. Please go back inside. Thank you."

The zombie at the gate turned toward the police car, a

small compact car that looked fast and mean. There were two officers inside. One got out, with a gun of some kind. The zombie growled and then fell to the sidewalk, twitching. The other officer got out and they both stared at her. Both wore the basic cop uniform, but they were clearly zombies, too. Zombies policing other zombies. Why did that seem corrupt and stupid as hell? The female stepped to the gate, her lower face hidden by a surgical mask. "Get the fuck back inside. Now. You stupid? Put the rock down, sweetie. Put that rock down or we'll shoot you, too." The female cop raised her gun, waggled her finger over the trigger. "Go on, now." The zombie cop let her toad-colored eyes mark Hannah, to put Hannah into her memory.

Hannah put the rock down. Hannah went. She dared look back and saw the two officers haul the other zombie upward and stuff him into the trunk. She saw the cops had noticed her watching them do that. The male took a cell phone from his pocket; the other just stared at her, did a finger across the throat gesture. Hannah got back to her apartment, and burst into miserable tears. She sobbed for a long time, just sank down, with her back to the apartment door. Pebbles came over and she sobbed into his soft fur until he wiggled away, clearly so done with her hysterics. Food, then another shower, and then bed. Sleep, where she could actually ... sleep. In a clean bed. Under clean blankets, in a box of safety. The apartment, just a small safe box. Why was she sobbing? Her nose hurt. Her face hurt. "Get it together, you big baby." She got up, locked her door.

Ice for her face. Maybe heat up those ravioli? That smell of bleach still strong but the cat shit smell at least had lessened a bit. Hannah stood, went to the fridge, and then opened the small freezer box. An ice tray, yes. Frozen meat paste. What was that? A package that just declared it was Frozen Meat Paste, Western Family Brand. No calories, no what was in it, no list of ingredients. Just a cowboy hat sitting on a happy-looking pig-bull creature. Someone had crossed a pig and a cow? Ice cream, Moose Poop. With a too-cutesy vaguely deer-like creature, also in a cowboy hat. Certainly no moose had antlers like a mule deer or feet like a horse's hoof. Moose poop flavored ice cream, Lucerne. Chocolate chips, caramel swirls, chocolate fudge chunks, cashews. Why all that would add up to moose shit just escaped her exhausted mind at the moment. No calories per serving, no list of ingredients, either.

Because zombies don't do diets, and they like their humans fat and slow, she thought.

No bags of frozen veggies. Just mystery meat paste and ice cream and ice cubes. She'd have ravioli and ice cream. She put some ice into a dry washcloth, then smashed it with a coffee cup bottom. Oh, that felt so good against her hot face, felt so good against her swollen eyes. Pebbles meowed up at her.

"You hungry, cat?" The cat indicated, yes, he was hungry. Or was it a girl?

The ravioli heated up in a saucepan. Hannah vowed she'd wait until it got hot before gobbling it down. No microwave. There was no microwave. Maybe it did something to the zombies. Fectos. Munchos. She ate spoonfuls of ice cream as she waited, letting it slide down her gullet in blissful swallows. Cold, creamy, ungodly sweet and real. Real ice cream. She chewed a chocolate chip. Her bad tooth complained but she kept chewing. Dentist. She could go see a dentist. The bland tomato sauce bubbled around the slimy squares of mass-produced pasta filled with mystery meat paste. Ah, maybe the mystery meat paste in her freezer was the same filling as the ravioli. Yum. She found a loaf of store-bought bread, sourdough. She hated sourdough. Nevertheless, with some cheap margarine, pretty tasty. A meal of ravioli, ice cream and sourdough bread. Hannah ate hugely, her stomach so full it bulged out. "Thank you, Jesus," she sent upward rather snarkily, but hoping there really was still a Jesus up there, out there, watching all this from his beach getaway. She had always pictured Jesus at the beach, wearing one of those colorful flower shirts, big loose shorts and flip flops, with long curly dark hair flowing in the ocean breezes. She took the butcher knife with her, put it under her pillow. A butcher knife always brings good luck! Someone watched her, she felt it, then the air just seemed air again. Her fingers took strength from that slick plastic handle. Butcher Knife Jesus would watch over her this night.

PART EIGHT: BREATHING

Hannah heard breathing, then someone shook her shoulder. She lay in a bed. Where was she? She felt for her hunting knife. It might be dull but it could do some damage. Her fingers scrabbled across a knife handle, not the right feel but a handle nevertheless. Her fingers gripped it. A voice, low, male, same tone as the Boise cop. That same 'don't you worry lil gal' tone. "Hannah? I saw they cleaned everything up. Hannah. Nope. It's okay." As she slashed out with her knife, she heard it hit the wall. "Everything's okay now, Hannah."

A cat purred nearby. A cat. Her belly held food. Her skin seemed clean and grit-free. Her scalp didn't itch and crawl with lice. "What a... What?" Her voice sounded weird and too loud. Her knife had gone bye bye. And then someone sat on the bed she slept in. A stench, that stench of slowly rotting flesh. How did they keep going when they kept rotting so? How? Up she sat, her foggy mind starting to give out warnings. *Don't panic. Don't scream. You're safe for now. Go along, Hannah, go along.* Her bedside lamp got switched on. Harrison, in a dark sweater and dark slacks. The muddy eyes on her, assessing her. He had even combed his dull black hair, put oil or grease on it to make it a bit shiny. Oh, how had he gotten in here? She had locked the door. "I must have... I was tired."

"Yes. Everything is cleaned up. Kevin will be found by the right sorts. Not found, so much as the right people will tell of his finding. Our little secret, my love. Everything is good now, Hannah. Your poor face. Why don't you stay home tomorrow? I'll tell everyone you had a bad fall."

"I did. Into Kevin's fist. Thank you. Yes... Um, those

two came back and cleaned up the floor. I saw a ... a man at the gates. The cops came and took him." She watched as Harrison tried to control the sheer irritation and annoyance at this. "I took out some garbage. He was at the gates, trying to get in."

"Don't even worry about that. You took out some garbage? You? Well, yes. That's why you don't go out after dark, even here. Sometimes we get wanderers who get in from the Eatery. A storm, a bit of fence or wall gets damaged... They're like coyotes ... if there were still coyotes. You didn't interact with it, did you?" Harrison sounded like a combination of a teacher and a politician. Or a used car salesman. That slick, well-rehearsed gurgling of bull and nonsense. A preacher talking about the end of the world. *Too late, already here, darling Harry.*

A zombie sat on her bed warning her about other zombies. Hannah swallowed an actual howl of laughter over that, because it seemed she might just start screaming instead of laughing. "No. I know better."

"Good. Good! Well, take tomorrow off, get some rest, and put some ice on that. I'll email Jodi about this, don't even worry. Daddy has this well in hand. If you need something for pain, go to Dixie. He's a good egg."

"Um... You say that a lot. Good egg. Are you fond of eggs or...?" She smiled, tried to make it seem she was flirting, not grilling him.

"It's just a saying. For good humans. Some of you are ... not good. Bad eggs. It's ... a lazy way of talking. You're a good egg. I trust you." He ran a gray finger down her leg, covered by a sheet, by blankets. Revulsion. No matter how nice this Harrison tried to act, he was still a walking rotting corpse. Some women might find zombie men hot and doable, she did not. She'd watched too many zombies chase down and then eat their prey. That had not been sexy at all. Real zombie behavior had been gross, disturbing, gut-wrenching, awful, and was etched into the frame of her brain for all time.

"It took some time for that," she said. "For you to trust me." How wearisome. To have to always be careful. Even in hell or wherever this was.

"Yes, it did. But tonight... You batted a homerun and called checkmate at the same time. It was the perfect time for Kevin to take his own life. I'm almost wary of how perfectly you timed this. I turned the DVD player off, by the way." Harrison got up and she heard the stretch of stiff tissues complaining. A whiff of his odor, a whiff of his strong cologne. Road kill in the summer sun and Old Spice Extra Smelly. "I know there are factions intent on disrupting our way of life. It's very tempting to let them persuade you to, well, get combative. There's a crackdown on that right now. We're all in this together. Strife and fighting and divisiveness are futile and a dead end. It's time to work together, Hannah. You don't want to end up in one of those Eatery camps, Hannah. I'd hate for that to happen to you because you let the wrong cute boy turn your head."

"So, you all are just nice Hitlers? Great." She bit at her lips for saying that. Cute boy?? What fucking fresh hell was this? Cute boy turn her head? Did he mean Kevin the Squeaky? "Just a joke."

"Who's Hitler?" Harrison's head tilted. He seemed as if he knew who that was, oh yes. Hannah shrugged, rather than launch into what she'd been taught about one of history's worst monsters. It might even be that Hitler had not existed in this reality, or hell, or heaven, or other world. Fuck, why hadn't she read more comic books? They were always talking about this stuff. Also, no sense giving the zombies any ideas. Apparently they already had ideas of what to do with bad humans who wanted a zombie-free existence. Oh yes!

"Never mind. I need to call Phil. She's, um, driving this month."

"You do that. Remind her about the Harvarti. Ridesharing, such a good idea of that Nora. Too bad Nora will have to be transferred to the Salt Lake offices for some training. She's totally botched, well, you know... We hope we can get her back again in tip-top form." Harrison left her bedroom. Hannah got up, gulping, trying to remember all that, to make sense of it. She put the knife back under the pillow. She heard the door open and close. He had a key? Hannah doubted Nora would be returning to the Boise offices. Hannah was quite sure Nora would be fed to corporate management in spinach wraps.

Phone. Where was her phone? Purse. The battery needed charging. Where was the charger? She looked through the kitchen drawers and found it. Phil answered after two rings.

"Hey, Phil. I won't be going to work tomorrow."

"Oh. Okay. I guess someone else can get that crackers and cheese."

"You bet. Havarti forever! Okay. Bye..."

"Are you okay? Have you heard? It was on the news."

Hannah filled a plastic tumbler with water. Clear water. Not muddy. Not full of floating human debris. "Something happen?"

"Jesus, Hannah. There's Fectos walking around, wild ones. And... Kevin. They found him. He threw himself from the Fecto Happy Tower. The mayor of Boise made a statement just a bit ago! Your Kevin finally went too far. That's why we have to be careful. It's... It's no good to go against them. Just no good." Phil mourned from the other end as Hannah rolled her eyes. Why did Phil sound so rehearsed, as if reading from a piece of paper? And how would that whole suicide thing get done so quickly and on the local news? Kevin had been cut into pieces and put into garbage bags.

"Yeah. Get some Havarti, that will keep the zombies happy. Havarti rules! We should all just lick their gritty assholes, you bet. Bye!" Hannah ended the call, thoroughly fed up with all this. She had been dropped into some weird office-heavy hellscape where everyone double-crossed each other all the damn time. She had never liked spy movies or thrillers. She had never even followed politics way before all the zombie shit had gone down. Havarti, eggs, havarti! Fecto Happy Tower?

What she knew: the zombies, now called Fectos, ran everything. They were in control and wanted to keep it that way. There was some sort of counter-group that worked against them. The Fecto Fighters. How tiresome. The Eatery seemed to be any area not under Fecto control. There were walls and fences up. The police worked for the Fecto control freaks. Wild zombies roamed about. There were drugs called Skeezies. She worked at some place called the Bureau of Humans. She had killed Kevin but the news said he had jumped from some tower. Living humans did not seem in charge of anything. She had a cat named Pebbles.

She noted she had several messages on her phone. Texts. She read one and her eyebrows rose.

We're on, K says it's a go.

What did that mean? K? Kevin? The king? What was a go?

K says you agreed to keep H occupied, so H can be eliminated, then u go to Chile. Deal? Han, respond? Don't get cold feet now.

Too much. Just too much. Her evil twin had been some

sort of stupid, legs spread to the world James Bond. Hannah plugged the phone in to charge it and toddled back to the clean, nice bed. She very nearly took another shower. Such a novelty, a shower.

Why hadn't Harrison tried anything? A kiss, a something? Oh, her suspicious mind needed a good long rest. Of course an enemy of the state, or whatever Kevin had been, would immediately be held up as an example of what happens to those who go against the Fectos. Still, this was a far better place than the Boise where zombies roamed like very murderous stray dogs, and there was no law, order or society left. Being free was not at all what it was cracked up to be—no sir. Also, where did the electricity come from? Were the dams on the Snake, the Columbia, wherever, still intact or built in the first place? Where could she pick up her mail? Did they have mail still?

Dentist. Look up a dentist. Did she have health insurance through her job?? Oh hallelujah if she did. She'd lick zombie bottoms for a week if it meant she could go to a dentist and have her bad tooth yanked for less than the national debt. No. No, she wouldn't do that. Maybe just nibble their nipples.

PART NINE: TWIZZLER

Hannah rolled over, hearing traffic and people passing by outside. Pebbles lay near her head. She didn't have to face that office today. Her face hurt. Her nose, broken.

After peeing, she peered at her face. Oh. Bruises and dried blood still on her skin. Shower! The spray hurt but Hannah knew that joy of having clean hair and clean skin would never become second nature again. She got dressed, in comfy loose jeans and a sweatshirt featuring, yes, cats of all kinds. Breakfast. She wanted sausage, cheese, biscuits, gravy, bacon, ham, eggs and... She wanted a giant gut-busting breakfast. She fed Pebbles, petted him. How strange to have a pet again.

No more coyotes. How could that be? Or maybe the coyotes hid a lot better now.

The zombies had eaten them, her mind supplied. Hannah got her purse, her keys, and left the apartment. An old lady, with a small brown poodle, stood on the small careful square of grass, looking out toward the gate.

"Oh Hannah, you're not going to work today?"

"Um. No."

"He do that, hon? Fectos, they can get rough. What can you do?" The old lady, with her mop of curly gray hair and her bathrobe, telling Hannah to just put up with being smacked around by a zombie lover. This really was hell.

"No, actually this was Kevin. He punched me in the face. Nice dog."

"He was a sonofabitch, a bad motherfucker, that Kevin," said the old lady in her sweet, high voice. Hannah watched the dog take a giant shit. "Dead now. The young always thinking they can change things. The young, so harsh and unforgiving. Little shit. He had the finesse of a butter knife."

"He sure did. Hey, do you know who Hitler was?"

The big blue eyes blinked, then the old lady shuffled closer to Hannah, as the dog scratched grass over its efforts. "I sure do, but how do you know? That's Before. You better not mess with that shit, honey. Have more finesse than a butter knife."

"I do. I hope I do," Hannah said and the old lady nodded, then whistled to her little dog.

"You can't play both sides forever, Hannah. Shit or get off the pot. You're in dangerous waters in a leaky canoe with a paddle made of paper tigers."

"Okay, thanks. It's safe to go out in the mornings, right?" *Paper tigers and leaky canoes? Maybe I'm the zombie here and everyone else is normal,* Hannah considered as the dog sniffed at a yellow bit of grass. She also helplessly pictured that dog turned into a soup, cooked in a big tin can over a hasty fire. How many dogs had she eaten? As many as she and Lyle and Jack could catch. Dog meat and dirty water soup had been a particular favorite with her and her comrades.

The old lady shrugged. "It's why we have gates and fences, honey. But sure, it's pretty safe this side of town. Come on, Peaches. Let's go get our housework done. I'm mopping my floors today and cleaning out my cupboards." Peaches, who did not smell like Sunni at all, lifted that doggy head, eyes focused on the old lady.

"Good. I need to clean mine out," Hannah said politely. "You're in 5, right? You moved?"

A careful perusal of Hannah, then the old lady shook her head. "23, honey. I'm in 23. Lived there for twenty years now. Since Yancy passed, Peaches here has been real good company."

"Oh, that's right. 23. I was thinking of someone else." Hannah stored that along with all her other odds and ends about her new life. Before. Before what? "Oh, hey, what's the code for the gate? The one I have doesn't seem to be working."

"76008. They haven't changed it since last year. Garcia decides that. You probably just punched it in wrong. I do that, all the time. Good morning!" She and her little dog moved off toward the second building.

23. *76008*. Hannah wrote that down on a receipt from her purse, for Shopper's World. Once out of the gate, she tried the code. The gate obediently clicked open. Okay!

No sign of that police-zombie struggle. She walked up toward the 7-11, after finding twenty-seven dollars in her wallet. The money didn't look quite right, but so what? If it worked, great. The man at the counter in the 7-11 looked up. A big white turban, dark skin, dark liquid eyes that came to her, and a friendly nod.

"No Twizzlers today, Miss Gray." He called out and then waited. The whole store seemed to wait. Even the woman, in light purple scrubs, waited for Hannah to respond in some rote manner. A smell of fresh coffee and hot dog water. Maybe meat paste water?

"Okay," she said politely and the cashier wilted, frowned. She felt truly bad. "Um... Maybe tomorrow?"

"Yes. Maybe tomorrow. Yes," the man said in his soft, fluid voice. He accepted a card from the nurse or doctor or whatever she was, ran it through and handed it back. She had gotten herself a giant coffee and a health bar. It just said Health Bar on the wrapper. Hannah went to the back of the store. The cold drinks on offer were either Coke, Black Cherry Shasta or bottled water. No beer or wine. No alcohol. The frozen food section held Falls Brand hot dogs and thick-cut bologna. With no ingredients listed. Mystery meat hot dogs. Ice cream sandwiches. Frozen dinners, about four or five kinds. Fish fry. Chicken-fried steak. Chicken fingers. Banquet brand. At least the brands seemed the same. No. Harriman's Frozzzen Treets. And yes, the meat paste crap. Ah. Butter, milk, eggs, cheese. All quite expensive. Milk, eggs and cheese would eat up most of her twenty seven bucks. Screw that. She wandered to the candy aisle. There were Twizzlers. What was the joke here? She saw turban guy watching her and she nodded at him, smiled. He nodded back then went back to tapping something into a laptop near the register. She took a pack of them, noting the price. Almost three dollars. For a tiny pack of plastic that tasted vaguely of strawberries?? She put them back.

"I heard about Kevin," said a man, whispering this as he ran his long fingers over the chocolate bars. Strings of blond hair against his narrow forehead, a small nest of whiteheads at the right corner of his dry lips. "Maureena sent us all a text. Stupid woman. What if... Stupid woman." He moved away, gave her a wink from one very blue eye, took his candy and a Coke up to the counter. *Maureena??* Hannah followed that winker and tapped him on his skinny shoulder.

"You're next. You're next to go. You're on the list, buddy." She said and was so gratified to watch that entire store flinch. Turban guy's rather lovely eyes went wide.

"But not you. Because of the Twizzlers. You're a good egg." She winked at the cashier, who gasped, then actually stepped back, against a blank wall where the cigarettes used to go. No alcohol or smokes? What did people do for fun? "Kevin deserved it. He got what was coming to him. He messed with the wrong bull. He fucked with the wrong hog." Hannah had not had such fun since... Well, ever. They were all scared of her. "Where are the smokes? Where can a lady buy herself a beer and some beef jerky?"

"Hannah," said the cashier. She noticed his nametag said Ajeet. How had he even come to be in Boise? "You have a nice day." He looked at the door and then at her, did this several times. Oh, hey, she knew that name. Kevin had said it. Ajeet!

"Where's the beer and the smokes?? Where are they? Why are zombies getting arrested if the zombies control everything? What's that about? Why does everyone care that some asshole who punched me in the face is dead? Why?? There are Twizzlers for sale! What's in the meat paste??" Hannah barely got a hold of herself, trembling all over, on the verge of tears again. "This is such a better hell than anything else. Why is everyone being such snotrags? I don't understand, I don't understand!"

"Miss Gray, come and sit down." Ajeet led her behind the counter, into the small office. He directed her to a chair. "I'll bring you a coffee. You seem upset." He nodded, then went back out, taking a phone out of his smock pocket. She watched as he spoke to someone, then let the phone slip back into his pocket. He smelled nice. Like cinnamon rolls. She saw papers all over: order forms, a list of what had come in, a work schedule pinned to the dingy wall. Kevin. No. Surely not the same one. No. Pull it together, Hannah, she told herself. A tiny button stuck to the wall that had FF on it. Just those letters with a line drawn through them. On a small round red button. White letters, a red line on a red button. A small metal bee pin, like the one on her purse, pinned to the bulletin board. "Here," she started as Ajeet set a small throwaway cup before her, full of plain black coffee. "I put sugar in it. No cream. Like you prefer it."

She liked her coffee with cream and sugar. Evil twin

needed an update on how to drink coffee. "Thank you. I'm sorry. I'm having a bad morning."

"A moment, Miss Gray." Ajeet stepped back out into the store and spoke to another smocked person. Then Ajeet came into the office, shut the door. "What has happened?"

"Um, well. A lot. This is good. Strong. Hot." She took a gulp of coffee, it burned her throat but it tasted like real coffee and yes, sugar. Lie, make up a lie. "I hit my head. I'm having problems with memory." There. Hadn't she watched a real movie, a while ago, about a woman who had hit her head and then could not remember anything? Why not? Sure. Didn't every woman in a movie act like she'd taken a blow to her skull? Too sugary coffee, such a good taste, a real taste. She concentrated on that.

"Is that why your face looks like poo and crap?" Ajeet asked, pulling up the other chair. "Kevin worked here so he could run the meetings from Dixie's tunnels and..."

"Look. I don't want any part in whatever's going on." Hannah interjected. *The same Kevin? That Dixie who had tried to inject crap in her face? The one Harrison called a good egg? Was Harrison also working to free the slaves from the zombie overlords?? Was there such a thing as a triple-cross? A quadruple-cross? Coffee good. Coffee real good.* "The zombies are fine. There's food, and showers. And working toilets. Ever tried to crap while looking out for zombies? It sucks. Everything seems great here."

The liquid black eyes regarded her steadily, with real actual sorrow. "No. No, it's not great, Miss Gray. We are pets in a zoo. When they can no longer find a use for us, they eat us. You are useful to them, Miss Gray. You tell them what we tell you to tell them, and it's stressful. I know. I know. But you cannot break down now. And... Kevin's death was unfortunate and a warning to all of us.

But it cannot break you. Break later, Miss Gray. You know what task I have. Do you see me cracking in public? I save that for private." He took her hand, squeezed it, then kissed her cheek, his lips soft, his cheek scratchy even as clean-shaved as he was. "We got three of them just from you tipping off Jodi and Harrison to a supposed meeting. Three. No doubt Kevin was taken in retaliation. That means we are getting to them. Such an obvious ploy as pretending Kevin's death was a suicide! The meat paste is a synthetic..."

"I don't care about the meat paste, Ajeet!" Hannah said at once, grim and hollowed out and shocked and a host of other emotions, most of which could be summed up with a good holy shit. "Maybe I killed Kevin. Maybe he attacked me and I took him out."

Ajeet sat back, watching her now. She suddenly sensed she should not have talked. At all. "Who are you?"

"I'm Hannah Gray. I need to go. I was just kidding. Kevin was supposed to come over last night and he didn't. Okay? We good here?"

"No, we're not. What actually happened to Kevin Taggart?"

"I don't know. Apparently he went bungee jumping. Yay! See? Kidding. I kid a lot." Hannah tried to stand but Ajeet caught her wrists, made her sit again. "What?" There were pencils nearby. And a stapler. And yes, a letter opener. "You want to make out? You're human, right?"

"Miss Gray. You're nice enough, I'm sure. But you've let Fectos have you. We can call them zombies in private, but be careful... I almost think they know about me. Do they? The truth." Ajeet ran his fingers behind her ears and into her hair. He's looking for wires or something, her mind supplied, even as she reached for the stapler to bash his brains in if this got any more awful.

"Sure, yeah. They know all about some nobody running a 7-11. Fuck off." She stood and brandished the stapler at him.

Ajeet held up his hands, stepped back. But he still seemed very dangerous. "I have frightened you. I am sorry. You speak like a Hollow. Sit. Put that down. Let us speak of all this."

"A what?" Hannah did not sit or put down her stapler. He stood between her and the only door.

"Sometimes people wake up claiming this world isn't real. They're hollow, confused, don't know the history or even who the president is. Rather like you, right now. If I didn't know better, I'd say you were an actual Hollow." Ajeet took a sip of the coffee he'd brought her, sighed. "But you know this. Zak, for instance. He just disappeared. He went around claiming the world got firebombed with nuclear weapons and the zombies were everywhere, that there was no law and order, that the world was dying. That he had died from cholera and woken up here. Died from cholera!"

Hannah glued her flapping lips shut. She nodded, kept watching Ajeet.

"If. If, Miss Gray, you are a real Hollow, you cannot let that Harrison or that Jodi know this, or anyone... Do you understand me? You were not that smart before, but you will have to be very clever now." Ajeet said with a straight face. Everyone thought her very stupid and as easy to spread as butter on a piece of toast.

"I have a cat. I'm fine. " Hannah put that stapler back on the small desk. "I hit my head. That's why my face looks like this."

The calm black eyes regarded her. She met them then glanced away. "Yes. That's best. Play the dumb girl role they all want you to, Miss Gray. Spread your legs and remember what the Fectos say and do, and remember what you are told to tell them. You cannot fall apart now, Twizzler. It's all going down in a few weeks. Hold on, Miss Gray. Hold on."

Twizzler. Like a code name? Really? She was some sort of superslut? A spy superslut? Oh god damn it. She had already messed all this up. She knew very well her patience for all this was less than half a second on every other Tuesday. "Look, Ajeet. Or is it Snickers? Or Marshmallow Peep? Is the candy the same? Never mind, just kidding. I'll hold it together, you bet. Thanks for the coffee. I'm okay now." Telling him her Twizzler days were done to his face might get her killed. She didn't have to participate in these zombie reindeer games. "I really want breakfast. What do you recommend?"

"Breakfast?"

"Yeah. Eggs, cheese, sausage. Breakfast. Oooh, potatoes. Hash browns. Yum."

"Breakfast. Um, the Shopper's World is pretty close. They'd have all that." Ajeet said and she nodded. "I have some milk, eggs and cheese here. I have instant..."

"Great, sure. But do you know of some great little breakfast place? Denny's or... What?"

His eyes had gone huge. His big soft pillowy lips had rounded out. "Denny's? What's a Denny's? Breakfast place? A place where we can gather and eat a meal together? Oh no, no, no. Those were outlawed! Those in charge claimed it was for safety concerns. Are you just kidding again? Miss Gray?"

Minefield. She waded through a minefield now. Careful or she'd blow off her own head. "I've been reading about them at work. I, uh, found this site. Nostalgia. Sorry."

"Of course," Ajeet said very softly and then ushered her

out of the tiny office and out of the front door, telling her Shopper's World was two streets over and then down Bailey Way. You can't miss it, he had said, his suspicious face letting her know he was on to her games but he had won. She walked back to the gate, punched in the numbers and went to her apartment. A car. She had a car. Pebbles greeted her, then went back to batting about a small ball. Hannah examined her ring of keys. The apartment key, a small key that looked like it went to a lockbox or a padlock. Ah, car key. Chevy. That did not help. Where was it parked? What did it look like? But… A real breakfast.

Did she even have a fry pan? Yes. A small one and oh, a larger one—both needed a good scrub. How much money did she have in her bank account? A list. She could make a list of what she needed, like a real goddamn person, instead of just grabbing mystery cans and hoping their contents did not kill her. Or trying to catch mice, then eating them raw because a fire would attract too much attention. Find her car, find the bank, then go shopping. She boiled some water for the beef Top Hat ramen and made coffee. Even slimy too-salty limp noodles tasted good. And having coffee again, oh.

PART TEN: YOU LOOK TERRIBLE

The old lady and Peaches were once again outside. "Hey, I think someone was messing with my car. Can you come check with me?"

"Sure," the old lady said, falling in beside Hannah, with Peaches on a leash, happy to be out of whatever apartment he lived in. A mother sat on a folding chair, holding a baby, looking glum. "Hiya, Bornia. Is he any better?"

"Oh hey, Maureena. No, not really. Hi, Hannah."

Maureena? Everyone was in on this weird spy game. "Hey, Bornia." What kind of name was that? Bornia shifted the baby to her other shoulder, patted the small back with a bored, somewhat annoyed expression.

"I saw someone by your car, too, last night. Maybe someone left you a love note," Maureena said, scratching at her chin. "You look terrible."

"A broken nose will do that to a girl," said Hannah. Maureena stopped by a battered, tiny, shit-brown car, the likes of which Hannah had never seen before. A little box on four barely functional tires. "This is my car? I mean ... it needs a wash."

"Uh huh. Yes, a ticket. Oh that damn, Garcia—he probably told the cops you were parked here illegally. He hated Kevin. I told you not to sleep with the apartment manager." Maureena handed the ticket to Hannah. 500 credits. Credits? "It's probably already gone from your account. You gonna appeal that? You do live here."

"Sure. I need to go to the bank anyway."

"Why? You went last year. The banks are theirs, honeypot. You looking for a fresh Fecto? You got a new assignment?"

"Yes, I do," said Hannah agreeably, already hating Maureena and her stupid brown poodle. Someone had trusted this old gossipy idiot with sensitive information? "You spread that around now, baby."

Maureena reared back. "Well!" She marched off, yanking that brown poodle with her. Hannah grinned and then shoved that ticket into her purse. Five hundred for a parking violation? When she lived there?? Who was Garcia and how soon could he die? She saw the apartment office door and went toward it, where an older man, fat and balding, sat doing something at a computer. He did not look up as she came in. He wore a dark red shirt and had hair sprouting from his ears. Glasses.

"What?"

A very low, belligerent voice issuing at her.

"Um, dude. Why did I get a ticket?"

"You know why. Don't fuck with the Boise PD."

"What? I... I didn't. Did you tell someone I didn't live here or..."

"Hannah. Shut up. I know who pays your rent. I'm not stupid. Get them to fix that, if you dare. I had nothing to do with it. Why did you approach that Fecto at the gate? Why? You know better!" Garcia took a long swig from a dark blue coffee cup. "Nothing gets you wetter than some danger, that it now?"

"Um ... okay," she backed away, confused and disgusted at what her evil twin must have been like. Or maybe her evil twin had also done whatever it took to stay alive. "So this wasn't you? It's five hundred credits."

"Jesus. That's peanuts to them. Get that skinny Fecto who comes over to pay it, or get it erased. He's paid your rent for the next four months. I'm sure you can lick something and pay this off, too."

No, stop, no, she told herself before she put her keys through his softer tissues. A key jammed in the eye, fun times. "Thanks for your help, Garcia."

He stopped, looked at her for the first time, his eyes a weird gray-yellow. "I'm not Garcia. What the fuck is wrong with you, Hannah? Jesus. Who did that to your face? It looks good on ya."

"I'm sorry. I hit my head. Skippy? Floppy?"

The man sighed, went back to typing. Typing what looked like a screenplay. "Funny, ha ha. You're another Winslow Yoakum." At her blank look, he sighed, took another sip of clear liquid from that coffee cup. "Nobody gets that reference. Cretins. He wasn't funny, either."

"So what is your name today?" she asked whimsically, trying to read what he was typing.

"Krakatoa Bullwhip. Whip, if you're daring. Garcia's got the day off. Like you don't know. Do you ever get any rest, Hannah?"

Do not jam your keys into this man's eyeballs. Don't. "I slept like a baby last night. It was great. So. Humor me, okay, Whip?" She smiled and he smiled back, so ready for mischief and mayhem. She very nearly liked this Whip, despite wishing to jam her keys into his eyes.

"Sure! Whatddya want? You never speak to me this long. You told me once I should bend over and blow a goose. I'm still trying to work out how exactly that would work. What's the haps?"

The haps. The haps? "Oh, just, uh... Where's the bank? And where do we go for mail?"

"The bank? Are you... You work at the Bureau of Humans. Too much fun with your zombie master?" Whips turned toward her, giving off a whiff of gin, and something like pizza. Not exactly pleasant but certainly nothing like zombie stench. He pointed at a wall full of slots with numbers on them. There was twelve. She must have a tiny key to open that number twelve slot. "Are you worried about that five hundred? Don't. I bet that Fecto that bangs you already has it squared away. Your banking stuff goes to them, so... You wanna check it? Kevin got the codes, we can check it anytime we want. Sorry about him." Whip winked and she leaned on the counter.

As he typed something in, Wells Fargo Americana something or other came up, with a, yes, smiling zombie stood before a bank vault. "I just type in your name and the code, and the account should come up... Come around if you want to see it."

She saw her name, a string of numbers and letters and symbols, then 1700.98. Whip tapped at that number.

"Is that to the good?" she asked.

"Yep. It's way more than I got at the moment. How come you won't give me a fuck, Hannah? I'm just as awful as the ones you prefer. Come on! Do I have to be dead to get you all hot and buttered?" Whip looked right at her and she sighed. Was she such hot stuff here in hell? In her other life, she had been an ordinary, dumpy thing and men had certainly not lined up to get in her pants.

"How about a kiss for helping me?" She offered, like something out of an old movie set during war time, when the men were men and the women were scared.

"Sure," he said, and she put her lips to his, let her tongue flip and swirl in his mouth for a bit as he grunted, his tongue gin-flavored, his hands hot and sweaty on her bare back. His hands had gone up beneath her sweatshirt. She stepped back as if she gave out kisses the same way some people gave out smiles. "Thanks. I got a stiffie now. Go away, I want to enjoy it."

"You do that. I'm going to the store. You need anything?" How wonderful to be generous. How wonderful to go out on some everyday errand like grocery shopping. She had memorized that code he had typed in. 65ggl. She wrote that down on that same receipt, alongside the gate code as she waited for Whip to answer. She also wrote down her balance.

"What are you writing? I could use lotion." The gray-yellow eyes crinkled and she shrugged, but smiled back. "Wow, your sense of humor get knocked into place or what? You never find me funny or kiss me ... mm. Have I been picked for that Long Vacation? Oh ... is that it? Are you feeling sorry for me? Am I going to Salt Lake??" He caught her hand, suddenly more like a little boy than a randy, foul-mouthed man with a rounded belly and fish-white clammy fingers.

"No, of course not. You're not going anywhere. Oh. Hey." Dixie had come in to the office, eyes averted from Hannah. "Hi, Dixie."

"Hannah," he said to her, before turning to Whip. "My shower isn't working. Can I get that on the day's list?"

"Yep. You need a new head or leaking or...?"

"Leaking. No hot water. Like usual." Dixie reported, before nodding at both, and leaving. Whip wrote a note on a clipboard.

"Wow, what did you do to ole Dix? And... And you'd at least warn me if you knew something?"

"Sure. I'd warn you if you had to go to Salt Lake. I don't know what I did to Dixie. Called him a good egg, I guess."

Whip blinked, cleared his throat. "That's their words. He prolly got spooked. You can be a bit spooky, Hannah. You let them bite you? They say you can't get that crap that way anymore, but they lie."

"Just the lotion? No Twizzlers?" She let fall and watched him grin, his teeth yellow.

"Ajeet likes his nicknames. No, no Twizzlers. I'm not a

power player. Send in Twizzlers!" Whip laughed and laughed. Damn, she was some kind of 'play both sides' superslut spy. "Watch out for him. There's suspicions now. Be careful. Hey, if I can find out your work status, can I get a blow job?"

Hannah went still. "My what?"

"How long until they send you to Salt Lake. To the camps there. Where they process us like hogs. It's what Salt Lake is really famous for. The Fectos play in whatever's left of Vegas and get samples shipped down... That report from District Four's Yellowturtle. You wept — we all did. We'd heard stories but to have it confirmed!"

"Jesus," Hannah said softly. "Yeah. Check my status. Oh hey, what happens in District Six or Seven?"

"You sure? Sometimes it's better not to know," Whip said. "I checked mine, it says ten years and five months. Ten years. But they lie, you know? They lie. You just kidding again? You forget we're it? That beyond here roams legions of Munchos? Or so they tell us, but they lie. Chile is far north of here, and listen to me babbling away to a well-used Fecto toy. I must be desperate. Check that or not, babydoll?" Whip tossed his head, licked his lips. She had turned dry as a bone but decided not to tell this information-dispensing sort that. Her evil twin superspy slut had done her a good turn here and helped her secure some intel needed to survive this new, hostile landscape. Hannah smiled, widely.

"Sure. Can you check that?"

He tapped and typed, and then fished a bit of green paper from a desk drawer. "It's all in one file... The Fectos have free access to this info but we don't. However, since you're being such a peach and gave me a stiffie... Ah, here it is. Gray, Hannah G. Hannah Gloria? Parents, huh?" He rubbed at his bald head with his long white fingers. An

Idaho man who didn't have a near year-round tan and didn't have farmer-rough hands? His entire lumpy body turned to lumpy stillness. That small mouth opened, she saw a bit of pork or chicken caught between two back teeth. "Fuck me." A whisper from the bottom of a slick-sided hole. The whisper of someone trapped, looking at whatever was about to kill them. She came around to where she could see the screen of his small laptop. "Oh, Hannah. Hannah."

Two months, eleven days.

There was her picture, yet it wasn't her. There were strange little differences. A fatter face, better hair, more makeup. Also, she wore a beige blouse and a string of golden beads. And tiny gold earrings. Reason for early termination: *unwilling to follow orders, sullen disposition, sloppy work, no real work ethic, possible FF agent.* There was also a star by her name, a red star.

Her mouth came open. Whip actually patted her leg, a friendly pat. "I'm so sorry. FF. Damn. They're thorough. Red star, that means recent. This was recently changed. Two months. Two months! We'll have to refund all that rent Skinny paid. Damn it."

"That's around Thanksgiving, right? Why would Harry pay that if he knew I was being killed?"

"Around what?" His eyes kept moving over the words by her strange, stiff headshot.. "Hannah, this is bad, this is so very bad."

God damn it. No Thanksgiving? They'd mentioned Christmas, Halloween seemed a real thing here. History had changed during her little self-operation. "Nothing. So. What do I do?"

Their eyes met, and his eyes actually grew moist, then tears rolled down his pale cheeks. "You run. I'd go today before they figure out you somehow found out. Go to

Chile, it's north..."

"Chile is not north. It's in South America."

"South of America? They moved it? Again?? That's so far. You'd have to fly there. The earthquake destroyed most of the land beyond Winnemucca, and the Fectos don't let us near the planes. Just go north, to the colony; it's there, it's real. The Chile Place. Maybe they meant chilly, as in cold?" Whip sighed, blew out air. Hannah wondered if this office was bugged, if the zombies had it wired. Paranoia, hello! "It's rough there, sure, but you won't get turned into food or whatever, right?" Whip logged out of the Bureau of Humans personal. "Kevin told us not to get careless at work. Dixie told you that. Just because you're a Fecto pet doesn't mean you're safe."

"Okay," she said, her head swirling with bits and pieces. "Who's taking over from Kevin?"

"I don't know. Probably Ajeet, he's as slick as they come. But Adam thinks he's working with the Fectos. If our group has any balls, they'll go with Irina Bella. She's a fucking shark and they're scared of her. She lives out in the Eatery, on the Idaho side. She's actually killed them, ten now at least. You met her that one meeting. Don't you think she should slap us around and make us all behave?" Whip wiped at his wet cheeks, shut his laptop. "You gotta get out of here, Hannah. Whatever you did, they're gunning for you now."

Shit. Maybe this was for Kevin. Maybe Kevin had been working for the Fectos, er, zombies. Maybe Harrison had done this to her, or that Jodi. But for not writing a fundraising letter? Surely not. She nodded as if considering Whip's warnings, words and wild tales of some zombie-free paradise with no running water, and probably everyone in tents. To go from a real apartment to some tent city? Named for Chile?? That just seemed ...

odd. "Irina Bella, yeah. Let's hope so."

"Okay. We'll get you safe. You're a good egg." He winked.

Her heart stopped. No. No, she was just being paranoid. "Thanks. I gotta go. I'll... I'll figure this out."

"Yeah. We will. We're in this together," Whip said.

PART ELEVEN: BREAKFAST

She got out of there. She went to her car, got in, and sat there clutching the wheel; the smell inside of stale coffee, and a rose-scented air freshener. A stick. She put the clutch in, shifted about, then started up the little brown beast. The engine coughed, missed, then coughed and decided to keep running. Music blared, something so impossibly syrupy and happy. She snapped the dial to the off position. She had a laptop at the apartment, she had paper there to write all this down to keep track of it. Ajeet, Kevin, Irina Bella, what really went on over in Salt Lake. Chile. Some giant earthquake that had taken out everything below Winnemucca? Was that a lie to keep the humans away? Who or what could she trust? Dixie? Maureena? Why had she become some double agent? She clearly had not been any good at it. Her evil twin had been both stupid and careless. That was a bad and lethal combination in a zombie-smeared world. Even when the zombies pretended to play nice.

Food. She still wanted breakfast. And away from this hive of busy bees. Her eye caught the bee pin on her fringed horror of a purse. Busy bees!

Hannah got the car, turned around and headed out to Montrose. The gate just opened. She must have something on the car... Yes, a little gadget by the speedometer that flashed a little red light. It must tell the gate to open, and yes, the gate closed on its own too. Almost no traffic. Two streets over and ... then what? She tried to pay attention so she could get back. Her gas gage stood at half-full or was it half-empty? Har dee har har.

Ah. Smiling Coyote Street, Ladywigguns Way... Who

was in charge of naming streets these days? Stoned cancer patients? Bailey. That had to be it.

Shopper's World proved to be a large supermarket that looked part of a chain. A big goofy sign with loopy, comical lettering, accompanied by a laughing cartoon lemon in the background; a lemon with those gigantic Japanese anime eyes... Yes, anime, that was the right name. A happy lemon that would go into lemonade and lemon pie and lemon chicken. Hannah parked, watched as mostly women went in and out of that big store. Carts waited to be taken inside. There were balloons waving in the gentle morning breeze. Tied to that goofy, trying too hard, sign. Big bright yellow balloons. Hannah wet her lips, then went inside, where it looked like a grocery store. There were cashiers and to her left, fruits and veggies, to her right, what looked like liquor for sale. With a man standing in front of the shelves of bottles and cans. In a Shopper World's smock of bright eye-watering lemon yellow. Ah, hence the lemon in the sign. The bakery at the back of the store. And no zombies here. She could not see any.

Hannah nodded to a young man in loose white jeans and a loose purple and gray t-shirt who headed toward the shelves of liquor. The smocked clerk took a small bottle full of a clear liquid from the top shelf and the young man handed over a card. Fine. Nothing weird here or out of whack, yet. She went toward the vegetables, potatoes. Fresh potatoes. Tiny potatoes in bags. Where were the baker ones? So much food, just displayed like it was nothing at all. Hannah's mouth filled with spit. She bit into an apple before she could stop herself, and crunched that sweet raw flesh, almost moaning at how good it tasted. She put three more apples into a paper sack, along with the one she'd bitten. One thirty-seven a pound. Whatever! Potatoes came in five and ten pound bags only. She took a five pound bag. Four seventy-five. The ten pound bag came in at seven-fifty. How clever. She nearly took a ten pound bag. Nearly. Why were potatoes so expensive? This was the Potato State. Well, the Gem State, but still, everyone knew Idaho rocked and rolled in taters.

An onion. Just a sliver of onion for her hash browns. For her eggs. She found yellow and purple onions only. No chives or Walla Walla Sweets or Vidalia's. As she did not like onions that much, she took a small lopsided yellow-skinned one and then she moved onward on her quest for BREAKFAST. Wait. No lemons. There were no lemons. Or oranges. There was something called Orange Paste. What the hell was that? She lifted a sack of it. Rather like Jell-O before you added the water. She read the back—add two tablespoons of water to one fourth a cup for your orange needs. Hannah put the Orange Paste back, noting it had a happy, big-eyed orange dancing on the wrapper. Orange needs? Who had orange needs? Who? Just buy an orange! Except there were no oranges. *Because California is gone and Florida fell into the sea,* she thought. Then she got a good long shiver that traveled from her groin to her hairline. She noted the rest of the vegetables seemed rather ... local. Nothing exotic or from sunny places south of the American border, or even from the Sunshine Belt. No mangoes or pineapples. No limes. She noticed a clerk in that bright yellow smock noticing her noticing the vegetables and fruits a bit more than just wanting to buy some Orange Paste. She nodded, he nodded. Another shiver. A big one. A warning. *Get some sense, Hannah!*

Hannah moved out of the fruits and vegetables. Why did it seem she had eyes on her? From all over? Because people kept coming up to her and speaking to someone they thought was the other Hannah, that's why.

A loaf of white bread. Penny's Buttermilk Homebaked Bread brand. Penny's. On sale! One and a quarter! She got a small container of raspberry jam which, according to an advert, was on sale. Saltines. Just white and wheat bread. No rye, pumpernickel, or fancy breads with seeds and fruits and nuts. Shouldn't Shopper's World offer more than two kinds of bread? No, three. Sourdough: Penny's Alaska Sourdough. Yuck.

Milk, eggs, sausage. Hannah headed toward the bakery portion, noting the other shoppers seemed very sad or subdued. *All this food and all this sadness? So what if the zombies were eating them every now and then? That's what zombies did!* Except... What if that two months was actually real? Two months to enjoy electricity and showers—oh, and real food and walls. What if she cleaned up her act? What if she became the best letter writer ever? What if she gave up her evil twin's freedom fighter ways? Oooh, bingo!

Was she actually considering placating a bunch of zombie overlords with her best slave girl routine? Yes, yes, actually she was. Unless she could transfer herself to another dimension or whatever had happened. The nice one full of oranges and no zombies. With wind chimes. A wind chime made of old tin spoons.

A box of donuts caught her eyes. Huckleberry and cream donuts. Long bars frosted with huckleberry-flavored frosting and filled with cream. She put them in her cart, even though they were priced at almost six dollars. Two of them for almost six dollars. Was there sales tax here? Two donuts. Not exactly a bargain. Sorry, but the stomach wanted what the stomach wanted. She'd jazzercise or whatever the current trendy exercises were.

Running from your zombie boss as he tried to rape you –
maybe that was the trendy way to keep in shape around
here. She saw the dairy aisle and damn, the eggs... Were
they made of actual gold? A dozen cost almost fifteen
dollars or whatever money was called. The milk. A gallon
cost almost nine bucks. Alaska prices. She had heard,
once, that Alaska had prices like this. What the hell?
Alaska had sourdough and absurdly high prices, that's
what she had always heard. If she wasn't careful, she'd
spend a big chunk here in no time. Breakfast might have
to become some mystery meat paste and some toasted
white bread. Followed by a fourth of a cup of Orange
Paste.

"What is with these prices?"

"I know. They're so low. We voted and got the prices
lowered. Voting matters," said a middle-aged woman,
who ran her fingers over the packages of cheese. Havarti,
mild cheddar, and American. That was it for the local
housewife's cheese choices. She had a dreamy, soft face; a
rather lovely woman with swirls of white in her dark
brown hair, and soft, dreamy grayish eyes that came to
Hannah. The woman clearly had been smoking some
funny weed or had dropped a monster load of the good
cough syrup. Her pupils were gigantic, her expression
one of utter, floating divine tranquility. She wore a plaid
mini skirt, a bright blue flannel pajama top, and knee-high
shiny black boots patterned with pumpkins. A too-slim
figure. This woman needed a mystery meat paste
sandwich!

"That's what I meant. The prices. Lower. Good."

"The chickens all got stolen but they got some more
chickens. I love those donuts they make here, but Dandy
says not to eat them. He likes me skinny and what Dandy
likes, I like. Want a Skeezie?" The woman dug slowly in

her snow-white purse, and then offered a single black pill to Hannah. "I took one an hour ago. After they took my baby away. 'Your baby is so pretty,' Dandy said, and then he took it away. He can't make babies. He said it will be raised with others, but I know better. "

Hannah took that black pill. She let it fall into her purse, noting there were mirrors and cameras everywhere. She noted that and moved closer to the stoned, too-calm woman. "I'm sorry." She made to go, after taking a dozen eggs and a small carton of whole milk, and then noted, in the mirrors that reflected the dairy aisle, that there were cops approaching her and the stoned to the gills woman. "Hey. Hey. Cops."

The woman sucked in her breath, her basket empty on her very thin arm. She stared at the rows of milk cartons. "Please help me, little bee. I live at 89 Parrot."

Hannah bit at her lips, but leaving this defenseless thing here seemed rather like leaving a newborn kitten out in a blizzard. There were two cops and one clerk — the same clerk that had been guarding the hooch. "Um, let me go buy this stuff, then I'll take you home. We're just two ladies shopping. Nothing illegal about that, right?"

"Yes. Nice," the woman said. "I'm Truffie. Truffilia. I walked here, I think." Truffie shuffled closer to Hannah as the approaching three came closer, but they were hesitating now. "89 Parrot. 89 Parrot."

"Shhh. Let's go." Hannah guided them both toward a checkout lane. Number three had a woman running items through the scanner. It beeped to show the item had been read, just like... Just like before. The cops now held packages of cookies... They were zombies. Zombies didn't eat cookies. Oh ... the same female cop from the night before. The recognition. The zombie cop remembered Hannah. Great. She got the potatoes on the belt, then the rest of it. She got out her debit card as Truffie hovered far too close, smelling of whiskey, urine and perhaps a laundry soap. The clerk kept glancing at the two cops and what was probably a supervisor as she swiped Hannah's purchases. She wore small copper balls in each earlobe. No one seemed to wear anything outlandish or colorful here in Zombia Boise. No dangly earrings, no bright neon half-shirts with bellies hanging out. Except those bright yellow smocks that made eyes water from a mile off.

"How's your day?" The clerk, Vitrona, asked. She bagged everything but the potatoes, took Hannah's card, and then let the scanner read it, too.

Beep beep beep beep. Raaaaaa. A receipt popped out from a small black box. Bright yellow, with vague lemon shapes in the background beneath the prices and items.

"Uh, fine. It's good. You need anything else, Truffie?"

"Dandy doesn't like me to eat."

Vitrona, plump as a young seal, made a slight face, but handed over the receipt. "Have a Shopper's World day."

"Okay, I will," Hannah said, and Truffie trailed her as the two cops watched, as the entire store seemed to stop to watch. She pushed the cart as the woman she had rescued stumbled in her Halloween-themed boots. She fell to her knees, her hair hanging over her face. "No. Get up. They're watching."

The two cops had come out and were striding toward them both. Truffie got to her feet, her left knee cut and bleeding. "Sorry. I'm so clumsy." That seemed almost as if the woman had decided to wake up a bit.

"Yeah, I got her. Thanks," Hannah said to the two cops. Their smell. Zombies.

"We can see to her, Miss Gray. You best go home and rest that face," the female said, her name badge said Hurley. Officer Hurley, or was that her first name? She had a giant handgun stuffed in her cop belt. It seemed excessively large. Cartoonish. The cops knew her name. That seemed off. Why would they know her name?

Truffie managed to look cataclysmically stoned and terrified. Hannah got the door open on the passenger side of her piece of shit little car. Truffie got in and Hannah shut the door. "Thanks, I got her. No problem, officers. We're friends."

Both zombie heads tilted at the same time. "I think we should take her home now, Miss Gray."

"To 89 Parrot. I don't mind taking her. Bye," Hannah got into her car, got the key into the slot, her stomach knotted helplessly. What had she stepped into? 98 Parrot? The two cops just watched as she drove off. Truffie had even snapped the seatbelt into place, her long legs crossed. The left knee dribbled blood a bit. She traced a finger through that blood. "What the fuck was that? Who are you? Are you in trouble with the Boise PD?"

"Dandy is head sheriff chief big cop there," Truffie announced with an angelic smile. "It's the other way. Are we driving down by the river? We shouldn't. Dandy said that's where the protests were and my eyes should only see nice things."

"Neato," Hannah got turned around, noting, yes, they were being tailed. By the Boise PD. "I'm gonna drop you off and then go. I'm already in trouble. I don't need this."

"No. Don't go. He won't let me talk to anyone. What's your name?"

"Hannah. Who won't he let you talk to anyone?" Hannah had a feeling this Truffie lived on the other end of Boise, the good end. Where the rich powerful zombies lived. "You walked here?"

"I walked a long time," Truffie looked out the window.

"Hannah."

"How far is this Parrot?"

"Miles. It's over by Gowan."

"Is Gowan the same? That's... Ah fuck, that's a long way."

"The same?" Truffie kept looking out the window, as out of it as a china doll on a shelf. "My feet hurt."

"Take off your boots." Hannah glanced at Truffie, who began to unzip her left boot. The leg and foot that emerged sickened her. Legions, bruises, cuts... Her foot was battered almost to jelly. The other leg and foot were in the same condition. This woman needed a doctor or a vet. "Look. I'm gonna swing by my apartment first. And uh, you can show your feet to my neighbor. You can meet my cat."

Truffie looked at her feet, then sighed, a big exhausted sigh. She glanced in the rearview, then turned her head to better check the road behind them. Her head came back around, her expression remarkably alert. "Take Westblaster. The cops will think you're taking the shortcut, but if you turn on Roosterhead, it will bring you back to Shopper's." Suddenly, the lovely woman had turned precise and cold.

"You're faking this?? Oh god damn it..."

"Please. I need help. I'm sorry. I had to act like that. I did walk there, I did. Just take the roads I said. It takes three Skeevies to give me a thrill anymore." The eyes seemed a bit shocked. "They took my son, okay? They took my son. Just get me to your place and I'll pay you. I don't think that fucking Dandy has shut down my accounts yet and I have cash. I have cash."

"Okay." Hannah took the roads, got back to the grocery store and then managed to find her apartment complex. The gate opened. It closed behind them. No

Boise PD. "You don't have to pay me. I just... I'm already in trouble. I got two months or something. I can't help you."

PART TWELVE: BUSY BEE

"Two months? What did you do? You look useful. Fuck. I just need to catch my breath and then hitch a ride to Chile. Okay? You got one of their pins on your purse. That's why I picked you. Did you just fuck me over?" Truffie gave Hannah a look that should have killed Hannah.

"No. What pin? Oh, that. That's just a bee. A bee pin." Hannah looked at her tacky purse, noticed, yes, there was a small enamel bee pinned just above the fringe. Black and yellow, something a teacher would wear to teach grade school. Her own grandmother would have worn a small cheap pin like that to teach. "I'm apartment twelve."

"Is it far?"

"No, it's the first building. I... I need to ask Whip about Dixie. That's the vet. He's a vet."

Truffie frowned. "Animals or army?"

"Animals," Hannah said. "Here's my key. It's just around there. Don't let the cat out. I really do have a cat, I guess."

"You guess? You don't know, Hannah? Twelve? If you double-cross me, I'll make sure they eat you while you're still alive. I watched that once. She screamed for a long time."

"I watched zombies eat an entire family, from the third floor of an apartment building right here in Boise. We good here?" Hannah said very quietly, her hands shaking. The pack of zombies had trapped the three in a blind alley. She should have shot those three to put them out of their misery, but the sounds would have alerted the twenty or so zombies to the fact that she was nearby. She had made the smart choice to sneak away while the zombies were occupied.

"When was this? Something like that wouldn't be allowed to happen in the open. It would be on all the buzzsites. The Munchos monitor those like hawks. Fine. I get it. You're a tough little bitch. Great. We understand each other. That's great. Twelve? See ya there, patriot." Truffie got out, winced as her bare mangled feet met the pavement, then she hobbled off toward Hannah's apartment. Without taking any of the groceries.

"Twatmama," Hannah muttered, then went to see if Whip could help. He punched messages into his phone, blinking rapidly, then gasped as she came into the office. "Hey. Can you call Dixie and tell him to come to my apartment?"

"Why? We got a new Humpalong. Top secret. Irena Bella, but it's a big secret."

"I need to talk to Dixie. We had a fight. He's not answering my calls. Tell him I need to see him. Please, Whip? I'll ... kiss you again." She puckered up her lips and Whip gave her an arched brow and a head toss, but she could see that idea appealed to him. "I mean it. A real kiss. With tongues. You can grab my ass. Whaddya say?"

"I say LET'S DO THIS."

"You call Dixie first and tell him to go to my apartment. Then ... you betcha." Hannah smiled, remembering too well the times she'd sold herself for dented cans of five-year-old chili. And being grateful she had something to trade for that chili. The chili which made her sick for days afterward. Kissing some desk clerk was no skin off her back at all, so to speak. Whip tapped at his phone, then listened.

"Hey, Dix. Can you run over to Hannah's apartment?" Whip listened to some spate of hysterical screaming, then shook his head at Hannah.

"Tell him… Just tell him to get his ass over there with his medical bag. It's my nose. Tell him that."

"Uh… Hey, Dix? Get your ass over to her apartment, with your med bag. Yeah, she's standing here bleeding. It's gross. What? I dunno." Whip looked at Hannah, then nodded.

"Just get to her apartment. "

"It's not locked, he can just go in," Hannah said. Whip relayed that, then hung up.

"Thanks, you're a peach." She let him maul her with his mouth and bruise her with his hands, his belly pushing against her, those pale hands yanking at her underwear even as his tongue tried to yank her tongue out by the roots. What the hell kind of kissing was this? "Hey, slow down. Let's enjoy this, baby."

"Shut up," he said romantically and then, yes, slapped her bottom so hard it actually stung. Hannah got away, and Whip remained alive somehow. She arrived at her apartment, carrying the potatoes and other bags, her mouth wishing she had never agreed to that very bad kiss. Her apartment door stood ajar a bit. She heard low voices from inside.

Dixie knelt at the woman's feet. Both looked guilty as she came in, staggering under the weight of the food she had bought. "Hannah."

"Just fix me up a bit and then get me to the pick-up point. That's all I'm asking. I can pay. I don't care about your politics," Truffie said, waving a fistful of cash at Dixie, who delicately swabbed at the left foot with a square of gauze and some reddish liquid. "Damn. That stings."

"It's iodine and some other stuff," Dixie said, swabbing away. "I don't know who told you that but… We don't just whisk anyone away who waves cash at us. Not in these dangerous times." He cast his eyes toward Hannah, who put the cold stuff in the fridge and the other stuff in the cupboards. She wished everyone was somewhere else. "You have money, so just go."

"Just go? Where would Dandy Roughhank let me land, do you think? Do you think he'd let me fly to New Boston?" Truffie settled back against the couch. "I need to disappear. Once you go to Chile, I hear, you stay there. They can't find it to kill everyone there. I can't pretend and smile and accept this anymore. I just can't. Please help me. Please."

"Wait... Dandy Roughhank, Boise's infamous sheriff? You're... No. No!"

"Yes. Yes!" She mocked him very well. Hannah enjoyed how very well Truffie mocked poor Dixie. "I'm the Fecto Megasheriff's lil gal! You got me! Now get me the hell out of here. "

"You have money. Use it," Dixie said. "You don't need us. You're one of them. Use your fucking money and get away on your own."

"I don't have anything, you fat little fuck," Truffie replied. "Nothing is in my name."

"Then why didn't you stuff money under your mattress for a rainy day, dear?" Dixie took out a small bottle, stuck a needle into the contents, withdrew it, tapped the needle, and then injected it into Truffie's left leg. "For infection and pain."

"I did not expect for things to go down as they did. For Dandy to treat me like some common ordinary human shitto, okay? Everything went numb below my knee. Is that what's supposed to happen?" Truffie looked over at Hannah, who had been putting her groceries away and wishing everyone was at the bottom of Lucky Peak. If that still even existed, of course. "I didn't want to live like this, okay? In a stupid little apartment, writing up happy happy..."

"Okay, we get it." Dixie snapped. He was now bandaging and stitching and puffing powder into that left leg and foot. "You never thought what happens all the time to others would happen to you. You thought their rules would never apply to you. Oh my! You poor poor thing."

"Hey. They weren't supposed to come after me. I did everything right. He's been making me wear these boots for a week." Truffie stared up at the ceiling. "Just get me to Chile. Dandy can't get me there. I need the freedom fighters to go get my son."

"That's not what they do. And how do we know you're not a spy? A spy would get hurt like this to infiltrate the Fecto Fighters. Hannah there is as dumb as a box of hair. She brought you home with her instead of taking you home. And..."

"Fuck you," Hannah said, and the two turned their heads, then dismissed her at once.

"She's the best I could do at the moment. I needed help. Dandy's watchdogs were after me."

"You should have kept walking," Dixie laughed, puffing the wounds with more powdery whatever.

"Hey!" Hannah came into her small living room, where both giggled over what a stupid bimbo she was. "How about I call work and report you both to Harrison? I bet he would love, love, love to send the army over here to eat both of you with a nice glass of Orange Paste. Yum! I was trying to help. I won't be doing that again. Now get out of my apartment, I want to make breakfast. A big, sloppy, bad for ya breakfast. Any cops come looking for you, I'll help them find you. Got it? Twizzler is done. Twizzler has left the building."

Dixie rose slowly, oh so slowly, to his small fat feet. Truffie sat up slowly, oh so slowly, her mini skirt pulled up almost enough to flash her expensive panties at one and all.

"It's not just Fectos that can take people out, Hannah," said Dixie.

"Oh, I know. I know. Now get out." Hannah went to her door, held it open. Pebbles waved his tail, looked out and then looked at Hannah. "The cat can stay. The rest of you can go to hell."

"Fine," Truffie somehow got to her feet, with Dixie helping her. They left and she slammed the door. Slammed it. Enough. Enough of the intrigue and being called stupid. *You are being stupid,* came her very next thought. *You can't piss off both factions. Or can you? Can you live somewhere in the middle and...? And not give a shit that the zombies rule nearly every facet of life here, and that people are trying to get free of that rule?* Yes. Yes, she could. Humans were not better at ruling others than zombies were. There was no improvement there. Freedom isn't free. *Well, no fucking duh. You just exchanged one set of crap for the same old crap with a catchy new name, hello!* Hannah knew there were some serious flaws in her thinking. But she did not care.

She had food, shelter, a shower that worked, a job to go to and money in her bank account. A cat. A car. She didn't have to spend most of her time hiding from zombie hordes or other humans that wanted to hurt her in very ancient and awful ways with new-fangled inventions. Or the same old knives and rocks, when the factories stopped making ammo and bombs. Security and relative safety for ... the idea that she could walk around free. Free. What the hell did that even mean?

Peel potatoes. Fry eggs. Make toast. That was her next order of business. She didn't give a hoot about saving this world or whatever Boise had turned into. Had she met anyone she had liked here? No, because they all seemed hellbent on some weird agenda. Zombies looking for signs of unionizing, and humans looking for freedom. Kevin had tried to kill her. Dixie thought her an idiot. Whip thought her a slutty idiot. Ajeet thought her a real slutty idiot. Phil wanted to keep her drugged on whatever Skeezies were. Sunni worked for how many sides already in this mixed up new existence? Jodi wanted that stupid fundraising letter to be perfect...Why were they soliciting funds if they already had all the money? That had never ever made sense to Hannah. *Why did rich people or rich zombies, have to go through the pretense of a fundraiser? Why not just skip that crap and give the money to whatever? Was it to rub the poor people's noses in how very poor indeed they were? Yeah, bingo.*

Music. What was there for music? She went to get her laptop, plugged it into the kitchen wall socket, and went searching for whatever passed for music these days. Ghostbird, mostly. And Jenna Mayburry, a folksy happy singer from New Boston. 'We're all just happy clowns,' crooned Jenna in a high wavery voice. There was a music site called Official Tunes that her computer went to easily. She had an account. Ghostbird proved to be a pop band that sang about happy clowns, too. The plastic thin voice of the lead singer instantly made Hannah try to find something else to listen to as she made a monster breakfast. 'We're all in this together,' crooned Ghostbird's thin, very white, very pale lead singer, as a woman wearing a bikini beneath a see-through housecoat banged the skins. Banged them gently and with ladylike twitches of her bone-thin arms.

Easter Candy provided something a bit grittier, so she let them play, and then noted a few selections of their songs morphed into selections from Candylane and Sally's Horses. All of which sounded like the same band. Singing the same song. About happy clowns.

The potatoes were rotten. And small. Hannah persisted and peeled about six of them anyway, then turned them into hash browns after finding a grater stashed on the highest shelf in her kitchen. She got the onion diced and added it to the shredded taters. The onion had also seen better days. They grew onions around Boise, in the olden days! Why would a local supermarket sell such crappy produce? Maybe because that's all there is and because zombies don't eat fresh veggies. Ah!

The smell of onions and potatoes frying. Heaven. Hannah sniffed the air right over the fry pan, the steam assaulting her skin, and then she had to straighten as her broken nose throbbed and complained. Salt and pepper? Ah, right there, on a tiny Lazy Susan. Along with Garlic Sprinkle Powder and Meat Paste Fun Flavoring. What? She wet her finger, tried that. It was just salty and slightly hot. Like something you'd sprinkle on popcorn. She had salt and pepper, garlic, and salty hot powdered stuff. She was not a cook or a chef or anything like that, so it didn't matter. Salt and pepper worked just fine.

The eggs. What the hell? She scooped two out of the pan, threw them away, as they seemed spoiled. She tried two more, they seemed fine. She got her breakfast onto a plastic plate, poured herself some coffee, and then enjoyed the stylings of a band called Wild Lamb, which sang about happy clowns. That first bite. Ah. This was so worth not getting involved in whatever political nonsense abounded here. Badly fried hash browns sprinkled with slimy onion bits and badly fried eggs! She always broke the yolks trying to turn them over. Her boiled eggs were either raw inside or turned that horrible gray weird color. Still. Fresh food. Pebbles came to visit her and she let the cat chew at her toes for a bit. It sunk all four sets of claws into her leg, kicked away, spat madly and then ran away, as cats do when they play. She heard the thump of the small feet as it raced about and then the scratch scratch of kitty litter. "Pebbles. Are you pooping?"

Her phone rang. A guitar riff. She went to see who was calling her now to call her a slutty idiot. *Harrison,* it said. Oooh. Hannah sighed, then answered it. "Yeah?"

"Hannah. I... I just got some distressing news. I can talk, I'm out getting a snack. That's what I told Jodi anyway." He sounded so, so, so sad. What would a zombie snack be? A finger? A toe to nibble? A scoop of brain on a saltine decorated with a bit of parsley? "Are you okay? I heard there was a bit of a dust up with the police this morning. It's already been reported on Fecto Fighter sightings, dear. I can't help you if you're being all rebellious..."

"Yeah, Harry, that was a mistake. I made a mistake. It won't happen again. I'm the happiest little letter writer this side of the Rockies. We still have the Rockies, right? They weren't swallowed in an earthquake?" Hannah took another bite of runny egg, balanced on a bit of toast.

She heard the mutter of traffic from his end. "The Rockies are still mostly there, yes. You and your little jokes. Now, do not leave your apartment again today. I know you're basically a kind-hearted..."

"I'm not. That ended. I'm no longer a kind-hearted anything, Harry," she said. "If you can fix my problem? You're right. I let that Kevin talk me into shenanigans. No more of that. Cute boys, yuck! I'm done. My legs are closed to the general public from now on."

"Harrison. I hate being called Harry. And... I don't

know if I can fix this. You sound... very strange, not yourself. Is someone there with you? You can't talk?"

"I can talk. There's no one here but a cat. I'm a new me. I don't give a shit about anything but food, my job and not making waves. Okay? Oh, and showers. I love showers! Also, I got a ticket. Can you fix that, too? I can park in the parking lot here, right? Apparently, the zom ... the Fectos, sorry, the Fectos, run everything and me trying to argue my case would just be laughable. You guys do run everything, right? Banks, government, cops, everything. So why fight that? Everything seems to be working fine. I don't care if you eat other people, I just care that you don't eat me. Literally eat me, that is, of course." Hannah could not stop babbling. It bubbled from her like rancid vomit. Her breakfast congealed unpleasantly in her belly. *Stop. Stop talking, Hannah.*

"Hannah. I'm coming over there. Don't let them know. It's okay, honey." He hung up before she could start screaming she was alone and trying to be a good zoo animal. The music stopped and an ad played. Something about Apparel by Kimmy and a sale on officewear. One word. Officewear. Then the music continued. Sunshine Babies with their newest hit, Happy Clowns. 'You love life, so honor peace, not strife...' went the first warbled line. Hannah started laughing. And then she threw up.

PART THIRTEEN: COOL AS A CUCUMBER

Hannah sat on her beige couch, trying to pull herself into some sort of functioning, cohesive whole. After all, if she was to survive here, she'd have to stop losing her shit and start fitting in. Write down all the little every day things she needed to know. Just play it cool as a cucumber, cool as a pint of Moose Poop. Could she break it off with Harrison? Could she do that safely, and not end up as zombie chow? Probably not. Could she tell the other humans she didn't want anything to do with their freedom fighter ways? Yes, that she could do. They'd probably try to kill her. What a mess her evil twin had left for her. Where was her evil twin? What had happened to the Hannah who lived in this ... plane? Was that Hannah sitting in an abandoned apartment, about to end her life? Or walking about on some pretty island paradise sucking down rum and cokes? Probably. Let's go with that one. Or maybe ... that other Hannah had simply stopped existing.

Hannah shivered, then noted that her blood still stained the burnt orange carpet. That Truffie's boots had been left behind. And discarded squares of bloodied gauze. And that empty bottle of whatever Dixie had injected. Numbagil, read the label. Really? Hannah put the boots and the gauze into a garbage bag, along with the empty Numbagil vial. The boots had a smell; a rotting flesh smell, a stinky feet smell. Had Truffie really worn these for a week? Day and night? Ouch.

Hannah returned to the couch, not sure what to do with her so-called day off. There were no books to read, no magazines, and her DVD collection seemed to be zombie-positive propaganda pieces. Jesus. Maybe something on the internet? Except listening to more of that syrupy same-sounding music just set her teeth on edge. A nap? Oh, where she could actually relax enough to actually sleep? She turned on the television, got it switched over to the channels. The news made her giggle. Zombies telling everyone everything was okay and under control. No world news. A report about a festival in New Boston. What had happened to the old Boston? As she had never been to the East Coast, the footage played meant nothing to her. If Boston had indeed changed a lot, then, well, it had changed. Ramalot Broadcasting Company. RBC. There did not seem to be any other news outlets. She tried the morning shows, as it was still, oddly enough, morning.

Cooking with meat paste and orange powder segments, and other powdered foods. She watched as a thin woman talked about making a family meal for four from Top Hat noodles with meat paste added, flavored with Salt Lake Salt. Served with sourdough toast and for dessert, a nice scoop of ice cream. "We're lucky here in District Five," the woman said right to the camera. Her eyes had been lined with a shiny purple goop. *The eyes of some fish in a net,* thought Hannah. "Ice cream prices have come down due to the generosity of the Ice Cream Kings."

Ice Cream Kings? Hannah went to look at her container of Moose Poop and yes, there was a small round label that read: Approved by the Ice Cream Kings for sale and distribution. Holy mama tits! Was that a gang? A business? A...? Oh well. Hannah returned to flipping channels.

A zombie-laced soap opera, which fascinated her. It made all the humans in the cast into outright rapacious villains. The zombies were victims and never to blame for anything. The other side was both powerless and powerful. The human women were just gold-digging obvious whores. They wore mini dresses so short their panties peeked out. With makeup so heavy they took on the appearance of, well, clowns. The zombies all wore beautiful clothes and wore wigs of astonishing beauty. Hannah tried what looked like a sitcom on what promised it was a comedy channel.

No zombies. Humans acting very badly and stupidly, however. Bilgore's Acres was about freedom fighters who were tolerated by the local police because they were so very stupid. The two leads, male, actually fell down a lot and had trouble tying their own shoes. When they wore shoes. The women on Bilgore's Acres seemed to be extra floozy bimbos on steroids. They ran around in their underwear and talked in a breathy, fake way, preferring the local studly zombie guys to the local human duds — tee hee.

And then, she came across a badly done grainy channel, called Housewife... Yes, Housewife. It seemed to be careful little blips in between recipes for meat paste loaf. The Snake River Eatery seemed to be under actual siege by American Fecto Rangers who were releasing wild Fectos into Boise city limits to create even more reasons to crack down. Don't fall for it, whispered the big-eyed reporter, a woman with wild kinky hair and actual black skin. *Don't give up your freedom for their bullshit.*

This little segment, after showing some footage of a zombie yanking at a gate, with zombies in military uniforms standing by a truck that had once perhaps moved boxes of produce from coast to coast. To make it seem the zombies had let that other zombie out to go nuts. To fool everyone into thinking they needed more laws. So?

Hannah, really? You're gonna live with this shit and just ignore it?

"Yep," she said. But she could not stop watching as that same reporter or whatever she was, gave tiny reports during the cooking segment of the Peg Burley Show. That normal-looking talk show interspersed with careful grainy quick whisperings about the Fecto Menace. The zombies didn't know this chick was broadcasting this? Oh come on!

It took nearly an hour for Harrison to show up at her door. By that time, she'd found the Truly Old Movie channel—TOM—that showed, yes, movies made in the time she knew. Bringing Up Baby, Guns of Navarone coming up next. TOM has all your old movie needs, read the little crawl on the bottom. Guns of Navarone would be followed by Old Yeller. *Wasn't that a bit too close to zombies? But ... no commercial interruptions. Just Cary Grant trying to deal with ditzy Katherine Hepburn and trying to get a bone back from George the dog. But... Wouldn't these old movies show a world ... the zombies wished to utterly erase? Or did this channel only show zombie-approved movies? Did TOM play Night of the Living Dead?* She laughed—she had to. He knocked again and she rolled her eyes, then put the movie on mute. "Come in."

The door handle rattled but she had not locked it. Harrison opened and then closed her door, wearing a subdued lime green and bright purple suit today. Why was he the only one who seemed to dress in colors? He cast his eyes about and she realized he was looking for her kidnappers or others of some kind. "Are you truly alone?"

"Yes. Shouldn't you be at work, sir?"

"Yes, I should. We're having an emergency meeting about you this afternoon. I need to gather myself, so I can defend you. Jodi is not one to cross, ever, Hannah. She comes from, well, those very high up. What are you watching?"

"Bringing Up Baby. Humans, right?" She gave him a smile and he did not return it.

"You seem remarkably calm, Hannah. Your face looks awful."

"Do I? My face will heal." She noticed suddenly she had not picked up all of the blood-stained gauze and that Harrison had noticed it, with his muddy slow eyes. They moved very slowly in the reddish sockets. "My nose was bleeding again." She gathered that up and then rose to throw it away.

"That isn't your blood," he said quietly.

"Sure it is." Hannah caught herself from asking stupid questions that would reveal she was stupid about life here in New Boise. *Zombies could tell what blood belonged to someone? Were they bloodhounds or something? Or something?*

"No, it's not. I know the smell of your blood, Miss Gray. Please tell me you didn't kill someone else. Please. You can't just go around killing other humans, Hannah!"

"I didn't kill someone else. I swear it. So, you can go. I'm fine. I'll be at work tomorrow. Writing letters or whatever I do there. Whatever I'm told to do."

Those eyes, in their reddish sockets, settling on her. "I have some time. Why don't you get naked. And prove your loyalty to me, my dear."

Hannah met the eyes, met them. "I thought you had to go save me."

"I want a reason to go save you, Hannah. I don't like the idea that you're just using me. I might be a Fecto, but I do have feelings. I mean it when I say I love you. I mean those words. I mean them," Harrison said in a quiet, still voice that managed to scream at her nonetheless. "I can ship you to the Salt Lake offices today, Hannah. I can sign the forms and you can be relocated today. I hate doing this to you but... Lately, your behavior is just bizarre. Since that breakdown where you threatened to kill yourself, that it was all too much." Hannah stored that away. Where was the other Hannah? The Hannah who belonged here? "Now get in that bedroom, take your clothes off and wait for me. Do you understand?" His hand ran over her face. His gray fingers that smelled like death and felt like cool rat tails.

"I'm not going to do that, Harry." Hannah moved back, smiled, noting that small table could be easily lifted and used. "You're paranoid. And you forcing me to play naked games is gonna what...? Wouldn't that make me hate you? Yeah, yeah, it would. So why don't you..."

"I'm not going to ask again, Miss Gray." Harrison let his arms dangle at his thin sides. His cologne filled the apartment air. His zombie stench did, too.

Fitting in here meant ... giving in to zombie bosses. In all ways. If she fought this or attacked him, then what? Try to get Dixie to help her after tossing his fat little ass out of her apartment? *I can't. I can't let this thing touch me.* "How about if I kiss you? And you don't..."

"Fine," he said very very quietly and then went to the door. And then he stopped, that wildly colored back to her, that dead-haired head lowered, his gray hand on that door handle. "Goodbye, Miss Gray."

Shit. Shit! Choose a side, Hannah. Choose it! "Fine. I'll be in the bedroom." Hannah snapped.

PART FOURTEEN: AFTER

After he left, with tender promises that he'd save her and she'd never have to worry about going off to Salt Lake City for retraining, wink wink, Hannah took a shower. She trembled all over, and no tears came. They were locked so far down, she doubted she'd ever cry again. He had brought her to an orgasm. That haunted her. She had closed her eyes and pretended the zombie doing things to her was actually her high school boyfriend, Manny. Manny had been an ugly left tackle who had died in a drunk driving accident his first year at Montana State, or something. She had so utterly loved him, of course. Until she learned that love could end as if it had never existed at all.

A scrubbing of her skin until she bled. Blood and water mixing as it swirled down the drain.

She sat on the floor of her shower stall, head down, skin raw, shivering at the absence of the hot water, which had run out quite quickly. Water gone, the drip of regret and choices made. The sound of outside life, dimly heard. *Oh for a giant bathtub or...to return to running from zombies who had old-fashioned ideas that humans were prey, not... Oh.* Tears after all. Big giant walloping sobs. There was no way she could keep this up. It felt like Harrison had raped her soul with his gray fingers and his cracked dry lips. I didn't bring the toolbox, he had whispered against her skin. No wonder suicide had become a way of life here in New Boise. No wonder. She did not blame that other Hannah one bit if she had swallowed a bottle of generic Western Family aspirin like one would swallow candy. Had she sat behind a locked door and done the same with a bit of broken vase?

What can I do? She sniffed, her broken nose now paining her for real. Get dressed, make a plan. Where could she go to be free of both the freedom fighter assholes and the zombie overlords? Where could she go? There had to be places where people could just live. Pebbles came in, carrying that small ball in his mouth. She had decided Pebbles was a boy. She decided that right then and there. Hannah dried off, wincing at how very raw she had scrubbed herself, and then checked the cat's plumbing. Female. Female cat. Did she have to be wrong about everything, ever? "Pebbles. Where can we go?"

Those lime green eyes regarded her a bit reproachfully. Hannah waited for the cat to start speaking but it just batted that little yellow ball out of the bathroom. And there was no guarantee that Harrison would, oh crap on toast, save her. She had to—gulp—save herself. How to do that? Sitting in that office for eight hours with the very zombie who had ... done things to her, was just not an option. Remaining here in this little boxy apartment which seemed the center of the zombie versus human storm brewing just below the surface of Boise waters—no thanks. The walls seemed soaked with death fluids and whispers.

She would need supplies and food. A tent. Weapons.

Hannah got dressed, pinned her wet hair, then went to find some paper, and a pen or pencil. She got the butcher knife, put it by her as she sat on the couch, and then made a list of what she would have to do to make it on her own. Her face hurt. She took some aspirin. The smell of her breakfast lingered in the air. What would she need to do to make it here, away from all this giant snarl of bullshit?

Now, she knew Idaho, she had grown up here. So maybe she could make her way up toward Idaho City, toward Banks and into the Sawtooths, and then go up by Sun Valley. Cold, sure. Lots of snow, sure. Bears, wolves, maybe. Unless all the wildlife had just ... gone away. When was the last time she'd heard a bird here?

Hannah lifted her head. No birds? She went to her door, opened it, looked out, checked the sky. Small birds sat in the little wilted tree. No movement from anywhere. People were at work now. Kids at school. *What was being taught at the various schools? How to submit to your zombie overlord kings and queens? How to make an entire Christmas feast from meat paste and instant noodles?* The laundry room, empty as the sky. Get in that crappy little car and just go. Empty her bank account somehow. Because she'd need cash if she was going to live in a hole she'd dug out and put a roof on before winter arrived in the high country. A hole that would have to have several entrances just in case the zombies found her, and then she'd need a place to go to hide if that happened. So she needed two strongholds. Or a rocket, so she could go live on the moon.

"No, don't turn chickenshit," she said and shut the door. Plans. She had plans to make. There had to be others scattered in the Eateries that were just ... living. Just minding their own business. Fishing or hunting for food, or perhaps keeping some pigs or a cow or a goat or some chickens.

They stole the chickens.

Who had stolen the chickens and driven the egg prices so far up? People living on the outskirts of Zombie-Boise, that's who. Her little collection of inner voices told her she was being dumb. *Settle down now, girl,* said one; a sassy gay black man. She knew that was slightly racist, if not completely racist. Racism had not gone away with the advent of zombies. At all. Zombies had been blamed on non-whites in that time she had come from, after all. "It's the diseases they're bringing in from those countries they live in; they're so nasty and dirty. People from shithole countries brought the zombie plague." Had that not been repeated by the orange-haired fuckface, the last president before the actual end times? Had there been other presidents? That all seemed rather fuzzy right now. The zombies, and everything else, had been blamed on brown-skins. The president had said it, out loud, on a microphone. Presidents all over the world had echoed that, as well as prime ministers and kings and dictators. People had cheered and then gone on a brown-skinned people-killing spree, ahead of the actual killing sprees of the zombies. The brown-skinned people had not just accepted that, of course. A tasty little civil war had broken out. And then the zombies—the Fectos, the Munchos—had munched and feasted and ripped and chomped through white and brown alike. End of civil war, beginning of the end.

"The Muslims did this," Jack had whispered.

"This came out of those Ebola caves," Lyle had whispered.

Hannah hadn't cared. The zombies were real; she didn't care where Zombie Ground Zero was, as Jack and Lyle so often fought over... When both had been alive to fight over such things.

But, other than a trip down memory lane—memories she now began to doubt were even hers—was she being hasty and stupid? Could she stay here and put up with Harrison's... No. No, she could not. Her entire body vomited at that notion. Did she wish to become some sort of freed fighter warrior of the people? Fuck, no. Just no to that as well. So, the only option that worked for her, was to find a little spot to occupy that drew no attention and let her live out her days. With her cat, Pebbles. Though, Pebbles would find herself turned into a meal if things got interesting.

She'd need water nearby, clean water. Cooking pots. A bow and a way to make arrows. Lyle had made arrows by hardening the end in a fire. But he had been training for a world-wide event; he had been a backwoods survivalist. Living off the grid, as he always called it, had been second nature to him. Or so he kept telling everyone.

A way to preserve whatever food she managed to gather, kill or collect. Salt. Lyle had used the ancient ways. Salt and vinegar and drying. Pickles, apparently, were more ancient than Jesus.

"You have to make sure it's sealed tight, that's what kills ya," Lyle had told her. "If it smells off or has a weird look, don't eat it. No matter how hungry you are."

Hannah began to make a list. She got on her laptop, looked up the wilds of Idaho. Nothing. She could find nothing on anything outside of Boise.

Whip. Whip seemed quite good at getting around the barriers the zombies had put up. He seemed, at the moment, her best friend in the world. But when she went to ask him about the surrounding areas, she found a woman there. A brisk, white-haired sort with crackling black eyes. "Can I help you?"

"Uh, maybe. I need to talk to Whip."

"Whip? Ah. Clarence. My son is not available. Ever. To you. Now go back to your apartment. We're forced to rent to you, but..."

"I get it. I'm trash. Okay. Do you know if there are people living up in the Sawtooths or the Bitterroots, or even the Steens or the Owyhees? Away from the cities. And the zombies. And the rest of it. That's all I wanted to ask. Do...do you know? Ma'am?" Hannah asked as politely as she could. "Hermits? Loners?"

"Get out of here. Out."

"Do you know or not? Just nod! Just a nod. Please?" Hannah put her head down. Alone. She was alone here, living someone else's messed up life.

"Ma. I can't find the... Oh hey. Hannah." Whip came into the office from a door that had to lead to whatever apartment he and his mother shared. "I got her, ma. See if you can find that permit."

Ma rose, glared at Hannah, then went through that door Whip had just come through. A slam. A framed blueprint of the available apartments fell off the wall and exploded like a glass bomb. Whip surveyed this and then Hannah.

"I'm sorry. I upset her. That's my fault. I was wondering if you could, um, answer some questions."

"Jesus, Hannah. We're about to get raided because of you. You bring that high-falutin' bitch here and then throw a snit fit? We got Boise's Finest about to descend on our heads." Whip came around to further finish her off. "Now you get back to your apartment. And hope your Fecto honey can save you."

"Raided? Whatever. She's with Dixie, if that's who they're looking for. Are there people living up in the Sawtooths?"

"Ghosts live up there, Hannah. You don't care that the cops are gonna yank about five or so off to be interrogated? I'm sorry ... EATEN. Eaten, Hannah. You did this..."

"Really? I made that woman run away? I... What is that?" The rumble of giant wheels on pavement. The screech of a giant metal box on wheels. An engine designed for heavy duty warfare. She had heard such engines in movies, and yes, in her other life, when there had still been an army. They had come lumbering through Caldwell, trying to go after the zombies. Big tanks with

US Army stamped on their metal hides.

A wail. A siren. The reverberations of a giant industrial engine, then the front gate got bashed in. She turned to see a tank nose its way through the metal gate; through what remained of the wall on either side of that gate. Ugly ochre war beast. It had Boise PD written on it. Yep. A tank. Whip grabbed her and she punched him. He let her go, clutching at his throat.

"Bitch," she heard as she fled.

PART FIFTEEN: BOISE'S FINEST

Truffie limped around, in the big white cell, with the steel bars, wearing a bathrobe, with her legs bandaged. Dixie sat on the bench, blinking. Hannah sat on the other bench, holding Pebbles. Maureena had been taken away, along with Peaches. They had not returned. Bornia patted her baby's back with a blank expression. Whip and his mother huddled in the corner.

"This is not happening," Truffie said for the tenth time. Hannah had counted.

"Can't you do something?" Dixie ventured. Truffie turned on him. He wilted.

"He's mad at me. Say your prayers. Oh hey, you, Twizzler! Yeah, I got an earful about you, honey. Wow and hello and hallelujah. Why didn't you tell me you were Harrison's little sex toy? I bet you survive all this and we don't. You know Harrison wants to run the city. You know ole Harry wants Dandy's fucking job, you..."

"No, actually, I don't know any of that," Hannah said. Everyone there just shook their heads. "Fine. Yeah. I planned all this. You bet." She cuddled Pebbles, who had nearly clawed her to pieces in that police car.

"Yes, we know that now, Hannah," said Bornia, patting her baby — pat, pat, pat. "Sure, I had Kevin's baby but do you have to be so vindictive?"

Oh my God, what soap opera nonsense was this? "What now?"

"I love how she pretends. Such innocence," said Whip's ma. "We all know whose baby that is, you tramp. You Fecto whoregirl."

"Look at her. Even now," whispered Dixie. "I hope

Harrison chokes on me. I hope he chokes. I hope he chokes on this good egg!"

Hannah stared at the tortoiseshell fur of her pet. She did not know any of these people but they were still fellow humans, even as horrible as they were. Why did this seem staged? Why would someone allegedly as favored as she was, be hauled off to jail to be eaten by the Boise PD zombie troops? Why hadn't they just eaten people in their apartments? Something was so off here, and it made her head hurt.

"Just shut up. All of you. Just stuff it. Why didn't the zombies eat us at the apartments? Why bother with a damn tank attack to get in the gates? That's ... weird."

Heads swiveled toward her. Eyes went wide, brightened. A puzzle, of sorts, to distract from their coming deaths.

"They'd eat us where no one could sneak a picture of their carnage," said Dixie as Truffie sat beside him. "Remember that apartment feast that made it onto that Apparel of Kimmy site? Instead of blouses, ripped open humans, and zombies bathing in their blood. Proof they eat us, proof they hate us."

"Yeah, and they tried to say it was a hoax. The Department of Humans worked overtime. They even raised money to help the victims. It was gross. We had to go along or disappear," said Whip in that storyteller way, where the voice lowered, and people drew closer. "That was just down the road from us, over on Frenchcat Circle. They're still cleaning that apartment. To this day."

"Why bring me here?" Hannah asked, her mind spluttering. She didn't want campfire tales, she wanted out of here and away from all this. "Wouldn't I be in on it? I'm not."

"Oh sure," Bornia said and everyone just nodded.

"Why would I hide it now?" Hannah asked, hearing what sounded like fans from far off. Possibly to hide the killing, or maybe to get rid of the smell of something. "I have no idea what's going on here, okay? I woke up here, yesterday. In that office. I don't know any of you."

Whip started laughing. "Oh sure. Good one. Trying to be a Hollow now, Hannah?? Good ONE."

"No. No, wait," said Dixie, perking up. "She's been off since yesterday. And Hannah can't pretend worth shit. Ajeet calls her an empty cunt. She's got one use only. But she seems a bit ... sharper. Just a bit." The brown eyes rounded impressively as they came to Hannah.

"She kissed me, let me kiss her," Whip said, and everyone gasped. Except Truffie, who was examining her fingernails. "I've been trying... Sorry, ma. Cover your ears."

"I know you get your dick wet, son," said his mother with a disgusted sigh. "You've got no power or position, so yeah, the little gold-digging twatmama wanted nothing to do with ya."

"That's just it," Whip said, patting his mother's leg. "She acted ... real friendly. Toward me. Like ... she actually saw me. You know? Like... Like it wasn't Hannah at all."

"Exactly," said Hannah. "I'm not some gold-digging superspy or whatever my evil twin is! I... I killed myself. Look, I have scars." She held out her right wrist and everyone had to have a gander at it, at the twisting faint pink lines that went from her wrist to her elbow. "The zombies were closing in, they'd killed Lyle, and Jack was one of them. I got myself to this apartment, barricaded the door with a stove. Here in Boise—except Boise was fucking demolished, rubble, nothing left. Nothing."

"Hannah never tells stories," said Dixie, winking at Hannah. "Why didn't they grab Ajeet? Sorry, go on. Make it real good. So we don't care when the Fectos come for us."

"You don't believe me?" Hannah had to ask and saw everyone there nod that, no, they did not believe her. "In my time, zombies didn't run anything. We killed them, as many as we could, and then, I don't know… We lost contact, no news from anywhere. I watched everyone I loved die. I just tried to make it through the day. Until I couldn't. And then I woke up at that office. I remember the blood flowing over my legs and everything going dim after I cut my wrists. I don't remember any of this life or any of you."

"She's good," Whip's ma said after a bit. They heard a dog scream and then nothing. "Bye, Peaches."

Hannah bit at her lips, then said nothing more. She petted Pebbles as Whip and his mother were taken away, both whimpering and promising to be good, to be oh so good. Dixie extolled his medical skills, his giant mustache quivering, his accent apparently real.

This is not happening, Hannah kept thinking. *I am not watching people be led off to be killed and eaten by members of the Boise Police Department.*

Soon, it came down to her and Truffie. Pebbles leaped off her lap and went to a corner, where she squatted and peed with a very ashamed face before coming back to Hannah. Truffie came to sit beside her.

"Was that bullshit to help them or get in good with me?"

Hannah turned her head away.

"Come on. It's just us now. We're off-limits. We're Fecto fucktoys. We're safe."

Hannah bit at her lower lip rather than slug Truffie. She got up, moved to the other bench.

"It's okay. I'll find a way to get free of Dandy. Sorry

about all your friends or whatever they are. I'm sure you can replace them. You have to be a really good actress to get away with pulling a Hollow con job. I'd work on that, honey. You might want to get a nose job now. That's not gonna heal very well. Though you can always wear a veil."

Hannah got up. She went to the older, far lovelier woman and slapped her; a great ringing open-handed slap. Truffie fell off the bench, lay there, blood trickling from her nose.

"I'm sorry. Forgive me. Whoops."

It seemed far easier to slap someone than sarcastically answer them back. It just seemed far easier. Though, doing both had its merits.

"I do forgive you, Twizzler. I always choose so wrongly. You need to work on your Hollow act. Just a tip from a survivor," Truffie got herself back on the bench, wiped her nose on the bathrobe sleeve. "I choose to go with Dandy and let him defile me in exchange for enough to eat. He wants me to love him. They want us to love them. Have you noticed that? They want our love. I can't pretend anymore. It's why I walked out last night, when he was busy cleaning up that Eatery breach. A real one, not one of their staged PR stunt ones. They want our love. Like we're dogs. I had an affair—I just craved someone who didn't smell like gone over meat paste—and got pregnant. Dandy took away my son to punish me because I'm not a thousand percent loyal. He still expected me TO FUCKING LOVE HIM AFTER THAT. To be the little loyal BITCH who licks his hand after he punishes me." Truffie looked right at Hannah. "I get why you betrayed everyone. I get it. I do. I've done it, too. Far worse, sweetie. I thought I could live with it." She spit a glob of snot and blood onto the floor. Pebbles tried to get through the bars.

"Such a pretty cat. So few pets around. They get eaten. Such a pretty cat."

"I really did wake up here. I'm not ... this Hannah. I'm not..."

"I don't give a shit, sweetie. Save it. We fucktoys can be honest now. They don't wire these cells for sound. They prefer we make our little plans and then eat us as we wait to be saved. You should have let those cops take me away, sweetie. Did you really need to kill all those others...?"

Hannah had no answer for that. No one believed her. If she survived this, she'd go away. And try to forget what her careless stupid actions had accomplished. Death of Dixie, Maureena, Bornia and Kevin's child; Kevin, Whip and his ma. Anyone else? A zombie came shuffling through the double-lock doors that slid open and shut on electric runners. The sound of locks unlocking. A zombie came shuffling through. Truffie kept her head down.

He wore dark brown trousers that looked made of silk and a long dark brown jacket with little sparkles of green and gold in the weave. A subdued dull dark yellow shirt and a badge. A cowboy hat, pale gray, with a silver band. Dull eyes that came to Truffie with a real angry hunger, and then went to Hannah for a bit, before coming back to the head-bowed Truffie.

"You in a bit of trouble, babe?" A low, gritty, confident voice. Hannah saw Truffie gulp and yes, felt an actual moment of actual sympathy for the woman. "Do I need to have you questioned about some activities, or do you just wish to go home and accept a few home truths? You took your boots off."

Her eyes did not raise, her voice as soft and dreamy as a cloud of butterfly wings. "I just wish to go home, Dandy. They took them off. They did it. I have more boots at home to put on. I have more boots."

"Good girl," he said and then turned to Hannah. Hannah's stomach had turned into an ocean of acid over that boot bit. Couldn't that zombie not hear how fake Truffie was being? Surely, he wasn't fooled by that? "Mr. Squack vouched for you. I see what he means. That Fecto Fighter leader do that to you, honey?"

Truffie shot her a single sideways glance. Hannah saw Pebbles, watched the cat try to get away from that strange zombie smell. "Yep." Her throat had taken on a slick of bile. She tasted old bitter wounds that never healed.

"Too bad he jumped from that building. We could have arrested him for ya. Come on, babe. Karba will take you home and sit with you until I can get off work here. As soon as the paperwork's processed, you can go home, Miss Gray." He did not have ears. There were raw holes on either side of his misshapen head. How do you keep that hat on? How?

The cell door unlocked and Truffie rose and left, limping and subdued. Dandy stopped her, out of Hannah's earshot. He said something in Truffie's ear, caressing her back as he spoke. Truffie turned to him, her face ... like something from one of those medieval drawings of a woman being burned alive because everyone thought she was a witch. In utter awful pain but still alive, still alive to feel it. A nod from Truffie and then the two continued through the double doors, and out of Hannah's sight.

Hannah sat alone in the big holding cell, with Pebbles draped across her feet. If she got out of this, she'd just go. Head toward central Idaho. Into what her mother had always called snow country. Better to freeze to death than this. Two days. She had been here maybe two days. And she had killed herself once before, she could do so again.

What if she kept waking up in other places though...
Trying to figure out the rules and the game and...? Maybe
if she let a zombie kill her, whatever this nightmare was
would just end in ... nothingness. No memories, no other
lives, nothing at all.

"Miss Gray? Let's go, please." The same officer who
had come for the others. She got up, with Pebbles in her
arms. The officer led her to a small office where, oh, Ajeet
sat, with Harrison Squack. Both looked very stern.
Another cop sat behind the desk; a zombie, a woman. She
had a wig on, bright black and curly. And giant yellow
eyes, like egg yolks.

"We don't need your testimony any more, Mr. Kumali.
Thank you for being such a good egg," said the woman
police officer. Armitta. Officer Armitta. She tapped
something into the computer on her desk as Ajeet rose, his
smell of cinnamon like a balm in the fog of zombie stink,
heavy cologne, and heavier perfume from Officer
Armitta.

"I am here to serve," Ajeet said, casting his liquid black
eyes at Hannah, then he walked out the front doors. What
side did he actually serve? His own, she answered from
far far down, where the truth lives like a cockroach.
Hannah sat on the folding chair, Pebbles trying to escape.
Officer Armitta actually produced a cat carrier and
Pebbles found herself caged, but she calmed down
considerably.

"You have a permit for that cat?"

Harrison produced a small folded paper from his
wallet and Officer Armitta examined it, then handed it
back. Harrison put it away, put his wallet back in his inner
jacket pocket. "Is everything in order? She was just in the
wrong place at the wrong time and helped someone.
That's not a crime."

"According to our records, she's a member of the Fecto Fighters. That *is* a crime, Mr. Squack. She's a known associate of the late Kevin Taggart. Dixie Conware. Maureena Flame. Everyone questioned seems to think Miss Gray here works for the FF. Nearly all of her acquaintance are on our watchlist. You just want us to release her back into the wild?"

Harrison leaned back in his comfortable chair, while she perched on a folding one. Hannah noticed that, she noticed it. "I do. She can go to my residence. I told her to break it off with Kevin Taggart and he attacked her, which set off this unfortunate chain of events. Your police commissioner's inability to keep his wife satisfied and at home is not Miss Gray's fault, and she showed remarkable heart by trying to help Truffie Dill. Did Miss Gray make some bad choices in who she befriended? Yes, she did."

Officer Armitta tapped something into the computer, frown lines cracking her forehead unpleasantly. "What a pretty speech. Anything else?"

"No," Harrison said, then he took out what looked like a credit card. Yes, a credit card. Visa. They still had Visa these days. "How much is the fine?"

The officer looked at the card, then at Harrison. "The usual." She accepted the card, ran it through a small machine, then tapped something into that small machine, waited, then a receipt bled out, printed on bright red paper, with a Boise Police Department heading on it. She put this in front of Harrison, along with his Visa card, and he signed his name to what looked like ten thousand dollars. He pushed this back toward the officer, who tapped something into that small machine, which printed out another receipt, also in blood-red, with white writing. Paid in full. And then she saw the word 'bribe'. He had just openly paid a bribe, used his credit card, for her. Why?

"They want us to love them," she heard Truffie's soft, defeated voice in her head.

PART SIXTEEN: SWANKY

Harrison lived on the swanky end of zombified Boise. 3498 Boise Street. The nearest street was Arroyo Grin Avenue. A giant house that smelled of ... him. She swallowed hard, to try and stop herself from gagging. Pebbles scouted about and she noted there was a litter box in the kitchen; a giant fancy kitchen full of shining silvery appliances, a black marble floor, and wooden cabinets. A set of dishes that looked Chinese. A teapot that matched those fancy red and yellow dishes, decorated with roosters and dragons. A gigantic flatscreen television set hung on the creamy wall. What looked like some actual fancy fine art hanging on the creamy wall, by the dark wood stairway. A woman in a filmy dress looking out over the ocean, two small dogs at her feet looking up. A zombie woman and zombie dogs. Geez. The living room, hard wood floors covered by scattered black rugs. A giant, low table set before a giant fluffy couch of dark creamy green, like creamed spinach. Creamed spinach fancy couch, please. Shelves that held books. A home office glimpsed through an open door, where Harrison could work his magic and do whatever he did.

"I have nothing fit here for a human to eat," he said and moved past her as she gaped at his fancy house full of fancy stuff. "Salli hides her candy bars from me."

"Oh."

Pebbles meowed from that cat carrier.

"Is that all you have to say, Hannah?"

"I won't ever help anyone again," she said, her eyes meeting the muddy ones. "Is there a bathroom?"

"I have work to do. Don't disturb me for an hour or so.

I need to calm down. Move some funds around. Sell off some stocks." He went to that home office, shut the door. She heard voices. It sounded like a newscast. Yes, the financial news and dangerous times for investing right now. Hannah let the cat out and then went to find a bathroom. Now that she was out of jail, her stomach wanted food, her mind wanted mindless happy shittycoms. She didn't want to think for a bit, and then she wanted to run away from all this.

Did zombies sleep?

How was she to sneak out? With a cat? Or leave the cat here. *Yes, just leave the cat here. If it came down to it, leave the damn cat here.* Hannah found a small bathroom, with just a toilet, a sink, and yes, a big bottle of Anderhallow's Men's Fragrance. She sniffed this after she had done her business. Yep, this was what Harrison wore. There had to be a big giant bathroom to go with this big giant house. Upstairs? She wanted a shower—her last shower, perhaps, ever. And as for food; she had been hungry before, she'd be hungry again. If you could choke it down, it became food. If it didn't kill you, it was food. That rule had become her religion. If it didn't kill you, it was food. She had balked at cannibalism. Lyle had not. They called it long pig back in the day, he had told her.

But he had found a freshly dead corpse. Not all corpses turned into zombies. There seemed to be no rhyme or reason to the virus, or whatever it was. Or there was and she was too stupid and slutty to figure it out, ha ha ha.

Yes, a big giant bathroom, warm golden-orange marble walls and floor. A truly gigantic bathtub that looked like a small swimming pool. A separate shower stall. A big double sink and warmly pumpkin towels and warmly pumpkin wash cloths. And thick double-ply toilet paper.

"Do you really want to leave this for trees, bears and snow?

He's not so bad! You can put up with Toolbox Daddy! Come on, girl!"

Shut up, sassy black gay man! "Oh, I'm crazy." She took a look at her face, which seemed even more swollen and uglier today. She looked at the sink instead.

Did Idaho even have bears anymore? Wouldn't a bear be more than a match for zombies, even a pack of them?

"He brought you home?"

Hannah screamed. That voice had come right against her ear. She put her hand to her thudding heart, turned, and saw a truly amused young woman, who had a small but perky set of breasts and wore a gossamer pair of thong panties that did not hide the fact she kept her entire self as bald and smooth as a boiled egg. A very young woman, naked except for those designed-by-a-sadist panties. "Oh my God."

"Did you think he'd turned me into a roast after last time? If you're gonna take a shower, don't leave wet towels all over, okay? And don't use up all my bubble bath. It's my favorite this time. Clown Dreams. It smells like cookies." The big brown eyes looked Hannah up and down. This nearly naked creature could not have been more than fifteen. Fifteen.

"Salli?" Someone had mentioned this. Another one here who acted like she knew Hannah. Why was some young girl walking around like an advertisement for a brothel? Or a soft drink?

"Wow, Hannah. That hurts. Oh hey, Daddy. I scared her. Got a kiss for your baby girl?"

Harrison looked from Hannah to the naked nymphette. "I sure do." He put his lips to the soft round cheek and stepped back. "You girls play nice. She might be here a while, Sallianna. Can you order her some food? Just put it on my tab at Shopper's World."

"Oh sure. I'd love to. I'll make a list."

"Play nice." Harrison left and Sallianna turned to Hannah.

"I mean it. Don't use up all my bubble bath. I don't care what Daddy said, I'm gonna order really expensive shit. We can have a party. Just come to my room when you're done." Sallianna hugged Hannah before Hannah could stop that, her arms wiry and her smell sweaty armpits and expensive perfume. The press of that nearly naked teenager set Hannah's teeth on edge. "I'm so glad there's another of me in the house." Sallianna let her go, beamed at her. "What's with your face? Daddy do that? He likes me to call him Daddy, and to spy on you, but I don't, not really. He says, 'Tell me what she says.' I only do that sometimes though."

"Sure, a party." Hannah wanted to lock that door. "I fell. My face. On my face."

"Your face is all fucked up. I fall sometimes, too." Sallianna trotted off toward a room at the very end of the hall.

PART SEVENTEEN: SALLIANA

After a long shower, where the hot water did not run out, Hannah got dressed again and then just stood there, head down, in the foggy room. *Get out. Just get out of here.* It was the only actual thought in her head. *Get out of Boise, get away from all this.* She could not stay here and pretend she was her evil twin. It had taken all of two days to get most of her apartment complex killed and eaten by the local Boise PD. How many in that weird office could she get killed and eaten if she went back to work? Whatever her work actually was.

Salliana had a giant room full of stuffed giant animals, a giant bed covered with a rainbow-hued comforter, and her own bathroom. A desk with a laptop. A flatscreen television set, with a cord that ran from the set to the computer. Sallianna lounging on her bed, texting on a phone. "They'll deliver in a bit. I hope you get your own room."

"How old are you?"

"I'm almost sixteen. Why?" A glance from those shallow eyes, then back to more texting. "He just keeps me around because the other Fectos keep really young hotties as pets. He's trying to move up. You have to do what the big-time Fectos do. Do you like apples? I ordered apples."

"Yes, I like apples." Hannah sat on the end of that giant bed. Soft. She sank, the fragrance of that comforter rising up, rising up. Roses. Almost sixteen. "Where are your parents?"

"Oh. Dead, probably. I was sold to Harrison. At the auction. He's not so bad." Salliana stretched out, her tiny breasts jiggling just a tiny bit. She had a tight, hard little belly and very long, oddly kid-like legs. Because she was a kid. "I was eight or nine. I don't know. You never cared about this before. You were a bitch to me. And you kept biting me. If we have to share him tonight, no biting, okay? I can bite, too."

Hannah blinked, then turned away. Nope, not even that grand bathtub seemed worth this house of daddy zombie playing with his captives. Nope.

You sure about that, girl?

Shut up!

"What auction?" It seemed the safest topic. "Can you get, like, old television shows? I Love Lucy or Bewitched or Buffy?"

"You mean that show where that blond chick kills vampires? Yeah, it's forbidden, but I know how to get around that... Just a minute."

"Um... Do you have to be naked?"

Salliana had turned on her computer and the television reflected this. She went to a search engine, called Cloo, and typed in Vaunt. The site required a password and a username. Salliana typed in HarrisonSquack8 and then a password, which the computer hid behind little dots. A list of television shows came up. "Can you hand me my robe? He likes me to bop around mostly naked in case someone important stops by. I don't mind. I'm like a statue, he said. I'm supposed to be on display." Salliana found the Buffy selections. "What season? I've made it up to three."

"Wherever you want. I don't care. Oh, Spongebob Squarepants. And Dynasty. What a weird, um... Just start where you want." Hannah handed the girl a filmy pink robe and Salliana put it on.

"Season Two. Epi One. I love it! We can watch Buffy

kick ass while we eat apples." Sallianna set the volume and episode one, season two of Buffy the Vampire Slayer began, after three short commercials. "You seem nicer now. Oh, the auction. Yeah. I can talk while you watch?"

"Oh. Sure. I should go get the cat."

"Cat? It's probably dead. Fectos and pets, just a no go. The shots they take and they still eat pets. It's like they can't help it." Salliana settled on the bed, hugged a giant purple stuffed rabbit to her now-covered chest. "I'll be right here. You want it paused?"

"No. I'll be right back." Hannah went to find Pebbles. She went down the stairs and yes, the cat came to greet her, arching against Hannah's legs. "Hey, kitty." She picked up the cat, those lime green eyes so warm and full of light. Pebbles purred and rubbed her cheek to Hannah's face.

"Hannah. Can you bring that cat and yourself in here, please?" Harrison said, opening his home office door. She did so, already planning how she'd find a backpack, fill it with needed supplies and walk out of here a free woman. "Sit. Give the cat to me."

He held out his thin arms and Hannah hugged the cat to her chest. *No, something in her said at once. No.* "I'd rather not."

"Hannah."

"What do you want with my cat? I can keep it out of your way."

"Hannah." He held out those thin arms. "Cat. Now."

"No. I'm grateful you paid that bribe. I'm happy to play zombie sex games. This cat is off-limits. I'm going back upstairs to watch some television with your underage trophy." Oh, she could not seem to zip her lip and play nice. "I'm sorry. It's just been a long day."

He moved very quickly. She had forgotten that zombie

speed. In movies, they were so slow. In real life, they could be so fast. Pebbles spit and twisted in those gray fingers and Hannah got shoved to the red and black carpet, a thick luxurious carpet. And then Pebble's head went one way, her body went another. Blood. And Harrison licking that blood off his fingers. Pebbles' mouth opened and closed. Her body twitched and shook. Hannah sat there as Harrison picked up that headless dead cat's body and bit into it. She backpedaled, just wanting out of there, but he shook his head.

"No, honey. You sit there and watch Daddy now. Did you think there wouldn't be consequences?" Blood dripped from his mouth. Cat guts spilled from that cat corpse. Her lungs had filled with tiny nails. He took another bite, chewed, the crunch of bones. His muddy eyes on her as she tried to keep breathing. He swallowed, kept eating Pebbles, taking his time, enjoying that feasting. Hannah kept her lips locked or the zombie before her would have killed her; she knew that to her core's core. Paws, the tail, not consumed. Harrison chewed the small head to tatters. The gleam of cat skull bone, the exposure of Pebbles' small pink-gray brain. Harrison sucked down that dainty bit of brain with real relish, licking each fingers clean of brain juice and brain matter. Watching her as he did so. "You may go."

Hannah tried to get to her feet. The world wobbled and she clamped down on her entire being, forced herself to get up and get away, the door closing gently behind her. The stairs. Her knees seemed unable to remember how to bend. And then a soft hand on her back and a girl's voice. "Come on. Buffy's on. The food's almost here. "

"I'm not hungry," Hannah whispered as Salliana got her to that big fairy princess room. Salliana pulled that rainbow comforter over her, the colors of the rainbow repeated over and over and over. Buffy fought someone in the dark, twirling and kicking, twirling and kicking. Pebbles. "It's just a damn cat."

"Yep," Sallianna said agreeably, now wearing glittery transparent drawstring pants which hid nothing.

PART EIGHTEEN: OTHER GIRL

It had to be after two in the morning. Hannah came awake with a start. She lay in a big too-soft bed and someone snored beside her. Salliana. The television played a Buffy episode, and the room smelled of apples. Salliana had eaten six apples. Get Pebbles and just go. Oh. Except Pebbles... Oh.

Hannah got up, glad of the small nightlight that lit the room. Harrison had not bothered either of them since eating Pebbles. Salliana had been so pathetically happy for company. Human company. She had giggled and shivered through many hours of a show from another era, not getting the jokes and references but liking the music and the people who pretended to be high schoolers. Confiding she had a mild crush on this one or that one. Munching apples and enjoying slices of havarti. Sucking down something called Orangedreme, which tasted like slightly cold monkey snot. With an orange aftertaste.

"He locks the house down at night." Salliana said and Hannah came back to the bed. "The other girl kept running away. He ate her and then put in a security system."

"What other girl?"

Salliana sat up. The bedside light came on. Her pretty hair had become a tangled rat's nest. "Brickie. She had skin like chocolate. She got mad if you told her that." Salliana got up, lowered the volume. "I like that to play all night. Then I don't hear anything."

"I get that," Hannah said, a cold dead ball in the center of her soul. She had to leave. She would not remain here, kept in a fluffy room, like a doll. There were worse things than being caught by a pack of zombies. Yes, there were. "What happened to Brickie?"

"She kept running away. She wanted to be free. 'There ain't no place to go,' I kept telling her. 'Chile, I can go there,' she said. 'That's something the Fectos made up,' I told her back. That's what Harrison said. And what if he's telling the truth? What if you get out there, and there's nothing but those wild Fectos? They don't get the shots." Salliana went off to her bathroom, peed, flushed, came back out. "So, Brickie, she ran away that last time and the police dragged her back here. Harrison and the cops had me watch as they ate her. In case I was getting ideas. They filmed it. They play it at the auctions. With Harrison and the two cop's faces blurred out." Salliana now sat at the desk with the laptop. "You want something else on all night?"

"No, Buffy is fine. So, you'll just live here, until that zombie gets tired of you?"

"Fuck! Don't use that word. Are you nuts? It. It will be quick. He promised." Sallianna scrolled through television shows, her face tight. "It's better than being sent somewhere like Salt Lake. To one of the factories. I prefer this."

Hannah watched as a very young girl tried to convince herself that her upcoming death would be nice and pleasant. That her life was normal. That she was lucky and was leading a good life.

"Wouldn't you rather try to see if this Chile place is real?" Hannah realized she'd gone from just wanting to go along to wanting to burn the whole fricking system to the ground and then taking a giant shit on it for good measure.

"No. It's not. There's nothing good out there in the Eatery. I'm gonna change to Charmed, is that okay? I love their clothes. They're so pretty, those sisters. I wish I had a sister. Brickie never settled down. I told on her constantly. I thought it would make it better, that Harrison would straighten her out. He's real patient with me. It's not so bad here."

"Charmed is fine. I never watched it. Witches, right?" Hannah said after a bit. Salliana tattled to Harrison; she was dangerous. Harrison had trained her to be his spy. Salliana could not be trusted. *She's a kid,* something in her scoffed. *She's a spy camera for a zombie control freak,* her own inner self answered back.

"Yeah, witches. Magic powers. You sure?"

"Yeah, go ahead. I guess I should go find somewhere else. Get out of your hair." Hannah went to the door.

"I don't mind. My bed's huge. You're not in my hair," Salliana said, as an episode of Charmed started up, replacing the Scoobies and Buffy's magical vampire-killing abilities. "I'm sorry about your cat."

"Oh, thanks. I guess I had it coming."

"No. He's just an asshole," Salliana said, coming back to her bed, curling up around that same purple stuffed rabbit, her eyes watching the three pretty sisters having witch adventures. "You want a Snickers? Harrison voted to keep making them back east. They vote on the candy. To keep us happy with them. They got rid of Reese's Peanut Butter cups, but we still have Snickers."

"Sure."

The two munched candy bars that did not contain nuts, and watched Charmed. Salliana fell asleep. Hannah crept out, spooking at the creaks and cracks of a big house settling down for a night's nap. She went down to the front door and saw, yes, a small box with a blinking green light. A wire ran from it to the top of the door. Another small black box, where a green light blinked as well.

Somewhere there had to be a place to punch in a code if someone accidentally set off the alarm. She went to the kitchen and found not much at all. A kitchen for show only. Not even a knife rack. Ah, a long knife in a drawer full of cooking utensils. She took it, the blade very dull. With enough fear and anger, it would sink just fine into goopy zombie flesh. They had speed and numbers, but they were soft. Rotting and soft. What doctor or team of nitwit fuckheads had decided that making zombies smart and aware was a good idea? Why? Perhaps because the world had been dying and it seemed the answer. Why not just kill the zombies? What if... Oh. Maybe it was like trying to live with diabetes. As long as you kept it in check or something. Maybe the zombies took some sort of equivalent to insulin. But they still killed and ate fellow humans. Just did it while running the banks and offices and everything else. Was that really the best option?

And just how had the zombies come about at all? Hannah had never found out. The theories abounding about that topic ranged from asteroids to the Black Panthers to the Ebola caves. There was a theory that the Black Panthers had somehow unleashed an actual evil on the world with their hatred of white people. That one had been very popular in Idaho. Another conspiracy suggested the zombie plague had allegedly come from a plot by the Illuminati. A plot by the American Taliban, the Far Right Conservative League, or whatever they had been called before 'Shit Got Real', as Lyle had so jokingly labeled it. That space of time when people began to realize there actually was a god-damn zombie apocalypse bursting forth all over. The survivalists had had kittens. Their weird wet dreams about having to actually live off the grid came true. Until they actually had to live off the grid. And fight off zombies and each other. Then, the complaints! Oh my! Before, they had complained about the evils of the government and had spoken of craving real freedom as they sat in the nice, soft, modern world, drinking coffee and eating pie. That ship had now sailed. They found themselves starving, dirty, attacked on all sides and unable to yell for a time out. Playing commando off the grid and fighting for survival at all costs had not been the joyous laughathon so promised. Even for those who had practiced for just such a thing.

Hannah looked in the sleek silver fridge and it held nothing but what Sallianna had ordered, and a bowl of raw chunked flesh of some kind. Not pork or chicken. Beef or venison or ... human. Something dark and bloody. She had seen zombies gnaw on rotted corpses, so putting some kind of poison in that meat did not seem feasible. *Kill him tonight,* something in her whispered. Take that knife and drive it through his rotty little brain. That spark of life that kept them going would go out if the brain got spiked with something. The movies got that right. Putting blunt objects into the brain of anything would kill it too. It wasn't magic, after all. Brains were not meant to survive blunt force traumas or stabbings. That was not magic or voodoo or witchcraft. That was just how things actually worked.

Hadn't she ... been considering that without actually considering it? Kill Harrison and then what? How would she get her and Salliana out of this house without that alarm alerting anyone? Into the big Mercedes he had driven her here in and then ... down the road. American road trips, as American as America itself. Head north. Supplies. Harrison had an account at the grocery store. Spend another day here, order some food, and then dismantle the security system and kill Harrison. Head north with or without Harrison's little trophy.

Or…

Kill Harrison tonight. Take what food was here. Get to the car and get going before whatever security forces got here, and just go like the wind. What if she found herself shipped off somewhere tomorrow? What if Harrison stopped trying to protect her and just ripped off her head? Her intuition and instincts had gone oddly silent. Her heart beat in her chest. Keys. She'd need the keys to that car of Harrison's. She'd need more than a dull knife for a weapon. She had no idea what had happened to the landscape, so driving blindly toward the mountains was probably utterly stupid, but after killing a bigwig zombie, well….

Hannah found Harrison's bedroom, where he sat watching some sedate news program in the middle of the eternal night. The door had been left open. The knife in her hand, her hand sweaty. That dead black hair that lay so lifeless against that still-goodish skin. The deep shadows beneath each sharp cheekbone. The tears rolling slowly down that one cheek she could see, the gray fingers rising to flick the tear away.

"Hannah," he said very lowly without turning, "go to bed."

"I didn't know zombies could cry," she said, searching for that awful, blinding anger that had brought her here to sink the knife into his brain. She felt nothing, nothing at all.

"Go away."

Hannah stepped into his bedroom, where a giant king-sized bed waited for slave girls and office workers to grace it. Dark blue quilt, pale blue pillows. A huge oil painting of a lake. A desk, a walk-in closet full of manly man's clothes. Rows of shoes, those expensive shoes probably handmade by naked nuns. Sink the blade into the brain and then go. Zombie tears meant nothing. It was far too late now to cry over a killed world.

Harrison turned his head only slightly. His left eyelid seemed inflamed and swollen. From something other than crocodile tears. "I know you hate me, Hannah. Let me pretend you don't for a few more hours. I can smell you. Salt and flesh. Salty flesh. Please go. I'm so tired of hurting you." He sighed, head falling forward, the back of his neck exposed to her. "I get memories. When I was not a Fecto. Playing with my dog. A Lab. Yellow and so friendly. She loved everyone. I'd throw a stick, she'd bring it back; she'd do that all day. It's what they were bred to do, bring things back to you. But she enjoyed it. Molly. Tonight her name in my awful head. Molly. I ate her. She was old and feeble and had lived such a long life, and I ate her. When the infection got me. I remember that, I remember that. I imagine you and me and Molly. That I'm not what I am. I love you, Hannah."

"Okay," she said and brought that knife down.

He had not been expecting her to attack him. Harrison gawked and crawed, his fingers trying to yank that knife that protruded from the top of his head. Hannah took the other chair, a folding chair, and whacked him for good measure. Harrison sunfished on the lush dark gray carpet, that sluggish blood zombies had spilling out in a thick crud, the tip of the knife sticking out just below his chin. She watched as he gargled, as he shuddered, as his hands fell away, as his muddy eyes peered up at her with something like gratitude. "Molly," his lips formed, as that sluggish black-brown crud dribbled from his mouth. Hannah stepped back and back, shivering, her eyes stinging. Her fingers found wetness on her swollen cheek but her eyes seemed empty of moisture.

And then he went very still. Then the smell of him …

the desecration that had happened to him. The tragedy of this man who had once lived and had a dog named Molly. She covered what was left of Harrison Squack with the dark blue quilt, shut off the small television relaying that sedate news program. Whatever God was left could now welcome him home, or however that all worked. Maybe there was no home left out there. Maybe that was why there were now zombies. Because the dead had no place to go. Maybe God had given up or maybe God really had died — whatever God was the real God. Allah or Jesus or Buddha. What did it matter? "For what it's worth," she said over the covered dead zombie, "I'm sorry."

Code for the door. Would Salliana know that? Maybe it was on a timer. It turned off in the morning and you had to turn it back on if you went out during the day. She needed the keys to the Mercedes, some supplies, another weapon or several, and water. Drinking water. Matches or a lighter to start a fire. If she could just find some magical log cabin high in the Sawtooths, outfitted for a life without electricity. Already stocked with gallon cans of chili, beef stew and peaches. And enough ammo for a small army. And a well full of good, sweet, clean water. And a giant trunk of antibiotics, and first aid supplies.

Hannah got busy. She ransacked the house for whatever she could find. The keys hung near his desk in his home office. The codes to the security system had been written down in a small leather-bound book full of important numbers, bank accounts and passwords. Harrison's phone. Right there on his home office desk. She scrolled through it. Calls to Jodi, to Sunni. To Ajeet. And one to Ulster in N.B. New Boston. She read the texts and shuddered at what she had escaped.

"Oh yes, she's young and will be obedient," had been one of Harrison's promises. They had been planning to

surgically remove her hands and feet so she couldn't go anywhere, and then put her on display. Harrison thought this a better idea than just killing her outright for ... whatever her evil twin had been doing? He had been trying to save her life. By mutilating her.

She disarmed the security. She gathered medical supplies and canned goods. She found a box of matches. She took a small Dutch oven she found, trying to be quiet and not wake Salliana. Salliana could just stay here. Hannah set her mind to just getting out of here alive. Dragging along some dead weight would just get them both killed, and Salliana would perhaps get blamed for Harrison's ending. As he was already, technically, dead. Getting Salliana blamed for that, well... It was a tough ole world.

Is it? You can't take the kid with you? Are you really going to leave this house with no defenses, where anything could get in and kill her? Are you going to add to this shit, Hannah?

"Yes, I am," she told that inner voice. Harrison had an account at Shopper's World. Call in an order, have it delivered here. Load it in the Mercedes. His cards would buy her gas if she needed it. And if Salliana were also dead, no one would find out for some time. It would give Hannah a head-start. That same inner voice trying to remind her of her own humanity squawked alarmingly at thoughts that turned so harshly toward Salliana.

Salliana lay fast asleep, not aware she was free of Harrison and possibly about to get murdered.

Yes, murder. It's murder, Hannah, that inner voice chided. *It's not killing a zombie, it's murder.*

"Killing a zombie is murder, it was once human."

Not the same, that voice shrieked.

Charmed played on the big television screen. The snores now and then of a child who had not been a child for a long, long time. Just put a pillow over her face and be done with it. Then order a bunch of supplies, get them delivered, then go.

What if there are roadblocks?

She would deal with such things when she had to.

PART NINETEEN: WHAT ARE YOU DOING?

Hannah took up a big, floppy pillow. The girl slept. The house would not give warning if something crept in the front door or the back one, or through a window. This was kinder. Hannah had survived for over a year out there, but there was no way Salliana would do so. The pillow went over the calm and distant face. Hannah held that pillow in place as Salliana woke up to her dying, as she flailed and kicked and tried to live. She struck at Hannah with her panicked hands, she bucked and bucked like a bronco.

Hannah frowned, her mind latching onto how the Boise State Broncos seemed very absent from New Boise. No orange and blue horses anywhere. No Bronco Nation decorations. Nothing at Shopper's World had been splashed with the Broncos.

Take the pillow away, Hannah. What are you doing?

It took a surprisingly long time to kill Salliana. Or maybe it just seemed a long time. Hannah held that pillow down, used her weight, used that knowledge that she did this to save herself. She held that pillow down. Salliana did not move. Her arms had fallen away. That humping and twisting of her thin body had ceased. Hannah lifted the pillow and then put her hand before those open lips. Nothing. She checked the pulse in the neck. Nothing. The bladder and bowels had let go.

"I'm sorry, Salliana. I'm sorry." Hannah repeated over and over, shaking. Her arms hurt from holding that pillow down. She covered the dead girl with that rainbow comforter. No movement, no breath. Just that slight shape that pushed up the too-colorful blanket. Get some blankets and extra clothes. Coats, gloves, scarves, hats.

The computer continued to play that long-ago series. Hannah shut it down and the room went dark. A house full of the dead. She got the lights on, trying not to consider what she had done and that none of it could be taken back. Call the store and have them deliver. Call in that Harrison was not going to work. Something had come up. Give herself a head start. Yes. The number would be on Salliana's phone.

Shopper's Way agreed to deliver her list within an hour, when she called at six. She found a winter coat in Harrison's closet. She found ski equipment. Ski gloves, a ski hat, a ski suit. These all went into the big heavy suitcase she had found. Along with socks. She planned to go up high in the mountains and it was cold up there. Harrison had not moved so he really was gone.

She checked on Salliana, who had started curling up into a fetal position. Zombies did not do that. So Salliana was not infected and would not suddenly come alive again to try to rip her apart. Or Salliana was playing possum. *No, stop it, she's dead,* thought Hannah, as she went through Sallianna's room for this and that. Socks, a coat, gloves, tampons, pads, bras... The girl had had tiny boobs. Hannah did not possess a large chest, but still. She found the box of Snickers, a box of twenty full size candy bars. Those went into the suitcase. Fat, calories—they would be needed.

Call into the Bureau of Humans.

Hannah found the main office number on Harrison's phone and dialed it. A cool female voice answered, not a recording. "Bureau of Humans. How may I direct your call?"

"This is Harrison Squack. I won't be coming in today,"

Hannah said, lowering her voice, doing a fair imitation of the defunct zombie.

"All right, thank you. I'll pass that message along. Can you be reached at home or by your phone, sir?"

"Not until later this afternoon, around three," Hannah replied, and then just hung up before she got unmasked. She'd take his phone, just in case. In case they were on to her or found him or the dead trophy upstairs in that creepy bedroom. She just had to wait for the delivery.

PART TWENTY: MERCEDES

The Mercedes started right up and she pulled it around by the back door, which was relatively hidden from the other houses. But no one seemed home. The house next door looked empty. A big brick two-story, with snowy white curtains pulled tight. The lawn had been clipped. A sign: For Sale, by Happertooth Reality. Excellent. The house on the other side seemed deserted, too. Or perhaps the occupants were on vacation. A three-story peaked roofed house, painted a dark red, with white trimming. Shades instead of curtains at each window. A thick white fence with a tall gate. Were they watching her drive that expensive, powerful car? Were the residents of that red house calling the Boise PD even now? Fallen leaves swirled by, in the bit of wind. Winter might already be a factor up in the mountains. If she slid off the road, it was not like she could call a tow truck or wait for someone to help her get that car back on the road.

She had to get out and get going, that was all.

Hannah got everything she'd taken from Harrison's house into the Mercedes. How had a Mercedes come to zombie-hell Boise? It was not fifty years old. Were they still making these cars over in… Where? Germany? You should get a four-wheel drive; something with a winch, a trailer and a machine gun mounted on the hood. You could get something like that in Idaho, tee hee. Had she not heard, nearly her entire life, how whackadoodle Idaho was? An Aryan Nations playground full of gun nuts, idiots and rednecks. Which, to be fair, was mostly true. Had they not come through her line at Target? Whispering about how the white people were under siege. Whispering about the Citadel and other reinforced places where white people ruled like tiny kings. Lyle had lived in the Citadel for a bit. Had found it too liberal for his tastes.

Shopper's Way was also sending over knives. Kitchen knives, but still. She would just have to find something on the way to ... Stanley. That was up the road a bit, doable at this time of the year. She could find some rich asshole's cabin and hunker down. An axe. She needed an axe. Wait... The garage the Mercedes sat in. Surely there might be more stuff to scavenge in there? Hannah went into that garage and found not much. Harrison did not play sports, he did not have fireplaces or a wood-burning stove, so no axe or anything like that. Boxes full of papers. And then she found a handgun. A Smith and Wesson. Loaded. Damn it. She needed a sword, a bow with a quiver full of arrows, an axe, a spear, and a club. But she took that gun. Five bullets, five shots. One chamber had been empty.

Salliana Nubbins.

The label had peeled a bit from the small white box, tucked up on a shelf. Hannah took it down, opened it. A shoebox. A receipt for Salliana, from the Tucker Auction House. Twenty thousand, even. Paid in full. Five years. Salliana had been five years old when Harrison had bought her. Dental and medical records. Female, healthy, no hereditary diseases. Parents had surrendered her by request. There was the name of what looked like a debt collections agency. *Stein, Sarandon, and Sander's Collections*, said the yellow receipt. Paid in full, Hiward Nubbins. Hiward? Was that a name? According to the Stein, Sarandon and Sander's receipt, the Nubbins had surrendered two children to pay a debt.

Salliana's parents had handed her over for settlement of debts. Plus a small cash settlement to the good. Yes, a receipt for that, too. The Start Over fee, as paid by the *Montgomery Groupers,* a law firm. This receipt was stapled in with the rest of the receipts.

Why go through all this? Why not just take whatever children the zombies wanted? Why torture parents like this?

Because it's more fun that way, her mind supplied.

Salliana's visits to doctors and dentists. A private tutor. Reports that educating Miss Nubbins should not be continued as she was of average intelligence and had no great talents that would benefit the Great Society. *She was human,* Hannah thought. *She deserved. She deserved to be treated like a kid and allowed to grow up and not get killed.* Tough ole world, baby. *Yes, it was.*

Hannah replaced that box lid and then put the box back on the shelf. She took the gun out to the Mercedes, put it in the glove box. Then she waited for the delivery from Shopper's World.

She also had a thought: *Burn that house down, with the two dead bodies inside. Start a fire in that kitchen. There doesn't seem to be a lot of neighbors here.*

Is that smart or wise, Hannah?

No, but it hides what I did, she told that voice, who had nothing to add beyond a *be careful* and *maybe try to build a bomb or something that can be detonated when you're miles away. Like on some movie.*

I don't know how to wire anything like that, Hannah told that very unhelpful voice.

And the car, she should get a different car.

Where? Do you see any other cars to take? Her mind seemed full of unhelpful suggestions and cotton candy fluffy clouds.

A delivery van drove up to the house, just like last time. The same delivery driver, a young man with pimples and short curly dark brown hair. "Hey. Salli home?" He held out a clipboard with her items listed and a place for a signature. So oddly normal. Those elk-brown eyes dipped to Hannah's chest then to her face. "You guys having some party? Nice nose, lady."

"Yes, a party. Salliana's not home today. Sorry."

"No probs, mama." The delivery guy actually said, then saluted her, before beginning to unload boxes and bags. She directed this to just inside the front door, deciding that directing Horny to load stuff into the Mercedes might be utterly stupid and self-defeating.

He smelled of a meat sandwich and limes. A bologna sandwich sprinkled with lime slices. Shopper's World didn't have limes. Cologne or air freshener then. "Okay! You have a Shopper's World day... I don't know you."

"Buffy. My name is Buffy Summers," Hannah said and the delivery guy nodded, winked.

"You have a Shopper's World day, Buffy Summers. Oh... Hey, if you get tired of Fecto cock, I got a real one," he patted his crotch and then got into the van. Hannah went and looked at herself in the bathroom mirror. Nope, she had not turned into some beauty queen. Same bad hair, same ordinary eyes. And bruises galore! Maybe Salliana and that delivery guy had done the nasty.

Hannah loaded the bags and boxes into the Mercedes. Canned goods, knives, lots of salt for curing — whatever needed curing — for winter. Camp-ware: a whistling kettle to boil water in, a deep soup pot, a fry pan. More matches. A hammer that had perhaps been sent for her to find by Jesus Himself. She knew she had ordered badly and she should have emptied that damn store into several eighteen wheelers and had them drive up toward the mountains as she followed behind. But this gave her a fighting chance. This gave her a necessary cushion against

... all this. She covered everything with blankets, made it look very tidy and boring. Anyone who looked into the Mercedes would not immediately call the cops. They'd just see blankets and bulges!

Harrison's phone rang.

Hannah checked the number. Jodi. *Sorry, he's dead. He can't come to the phone right now.* She let it go to voice mail.

A shower, then start a fire, then go. Last shower and working bathroom for a long, long time. Why not just stay here, in this house? Tell them Harrison went away suddenly. And who would miss some stupid trophy walking around in see-through panties? Well, the local delivery guys, but still.

Oh yes, stay here, at the scene of two crimes. And just wait to get discovered. Fun!

Run off into the wilds of Idaho and wait to get caught — also fun.

If there was even anything wild or mountainous left. If only she could know for sure. One way or another. Ajeet. She found her own phone, scrolled down to his name. He answered, sounding slightly drunk.

"Hannah? Are you still alive? What do you want now? All dead. They're all dead."

"Are there mountains left in Idaho? Like. Up around Stanley? Or Idaho City?"

Ajeet snorted. "You called me to talk about mountains? Am I being watched? You know I work for them. I already do their dirty shit, Hannah." The sound of him swallowing something. "Where are you?"

"Oh I'm around. Just. Just do you know if the mountains are still there?"

"Yea, they're there! That's where the ghosts are. Fuck, Hannah! I messed up, okay? I chose to live! I'm not brave. I'm not brave at all," he whispered and then started sobbing. She rolled her eyes and hung up. That was something of an answer. Ghosts. She'd take ghosts over zombies, oh yes.

Hannah wadded up a bunch of Harrison's papers in the oven. She filled that oven full of papers and aerosol cans. And then lit the bottom layer of wadded up reports on fringe groups spreading truth about Fecto activities. She made it out to the car before a muffled whump sounded, like a gunshot fired into a beanbag. The crackle of flames. Looking through the kitchen door, she saw her little effort at arson had taken off. More cans blew. The wall now had flames licking up it.

Off she drove, toward Idaho City, up Highway 22.

PART TWENTY-ONE: THAT'S WHERE THE GHOSTS ARE

The gas station proved quite easy. She had Harrison's gas card, which just said Gas Card, on it, and it was apparently a 'buy whatever you want' kinda credit card. She bought extra gas, telling the girl at the counter she was doing deliveries for Mr. Squack. She was on official Bureau of Human business. Which the dull-eyed girl had nodded at, swiping the card without questioning Hannah at all.

Gowan Road. Highway 21. Still the same. The cutesy-creepy namers had not gotten here yet. She turned toward the highway that went through tiny Idaho City. Flat tire. What if she got a flat tire? She drove toward the Lucky Peak reservoir, toward central Idaho. She noted the houses that had been going in during her actual life now seemed missing. Giant craters. She noted big giant houses out this way, but they looked deserted. One even looked like a castle. Perhaps that was where Dandy and his desperate boot-wearing sweetie lived. She flashed by the road that turned toward the castle. Parrot. Yes indeedy. Truffie was probably inside that gloomy giant thing, being punished.

So, she'd drive until she ran out of gas. That was her plan. Just find a place to hole up in, barricade and fix. That was her plan. And then live as best she could, away from all that Boise crap. Free of others. She had grown out of her need to be around people during that year of trying to survive zombies and the end of everything she knew. And she had no ties here in this new life. Murderer. That was one of her new titles here in New Boise. She had died once. If she had to, she could die again. But she'd at least try to live. And it was not like she could return to Boise. She had killed a big-time zombie and that poor Salliana. And squeaky Kevin! Such actions were probably enough to get her a public devouring by a group of Boise zombies during the ten o'clock news. Not to mention all those people from that apartment complex. Her conscience gave tiny twinges. She felt bad about not feeling worse. What had happened to her? Oh yes, she had watched the world explode and get covered with actual goddamn zombies. Such happenings tended to turn a woman slightly bonkers. And turn a woman into Charles Starkweather. Who? Some name that had floated across her mind's blank movie screen. A blast from the maybe past. Some guy who had killed people. Some guy, her mind mumbled at her in an inner voice that sounded like her mother.

Thanks, mom!

You're welcome, dear, returned that inner mom voice.

Hannah came around a sharp, blind corner and stood on the brakes. A wall had been dropped across that cracked, pot-holed road. With a guard on it. She very nearly took out the small hut and the guard ran out, yelling at her. He wore the outfit of some mega-soldier. He came right to her window and she rolled it down. "You idiot, what's wrong with you? Do you have a pass? A pass?" He stank, it smacked her nostrils. No cologne used to hide that stanky stank of a stankalicious stank.

"Oh sure," Hannah said, smiling, as she fumbled her gun out of the glove box and then shot the Fecto guard in the face. He went down, shuddering, that molasses-slow crud that passed for zombie blood creeping out over the blacktop. Hannah got out, undid that gate and yanked it open; birds calling, no traffic heard at all. She went into the little guard hut. A cooler, red and white. Inside were chunks of raw meat. Hannah doubted it was beef or venison. A laptop. A tiny generator hooked to that laptop. He had been watching a movie called Dog's Summer. She checked the local news sites and found nothing on her morning activities. Yet. A stack of memos, warnings about those trying to slip pass. To let no one through who did not have a pass. And a memo about wearing a men's fragrance just in case. Just in case? *Ignored that one*, she thought, slapping her knee for good measure.

Honestly, there was not much to scavenge in the guard's little metal hut. She took one of the passes, stamped with City of Boise's official seal—a brain drawn with a happy smile, hovering above a pine tree drawn with a happy smile—and wrote her name on the line. Just in case there were other checkpoints. She'd drive slow and careful. How far up did the City of Boise care about? Or have guarded? The wall went up and over the hills on either side. She heard the slow slide of feet and noted, yes, a wild zombie had come to investigate the stopped Mercedes and the fallen comrade. That shot had drawn scavengers. This wild zombie grunted and moaned as it shuffled along, one arm shredded to the bone, wearing the remains of a bathrobe. One flaccid breast hung down, with a dull crater working its way downward toward the black-looking nipple. The zombie carefully inched toward the hut, waiting, then inching some more, waiting, then inching onward some more. As if the now-dead guard had taken potshots at it and the zombie had ... learned. Learned not to just rush the hut. Yes, there were three gunshot wounds. One in the shoulder, two in the upper left thigh. The inching nearer zombie had its jaws open.

Are you going to stand here and wait for that thing to reach you, dear Hannah?

Hannah got back into the car, taking the gun and the

baton. The zombie clawed at the door of the Mercedes, grunting as the grayish fingers tried to get to the tasty living bit of candy sitting in the car. Hannah gunned that car and in the rearview mirror, saw that zombie stare down at what remained of its arm, before it turned to the zombie guard Hannah had shot in the face. The highway awaited her and she drove onward, slowing down to a sedate thirty miles an hour, which made the back of her neck itch. Because at this speed, they'd catch up with her. They were coming, of course, and if she didn't hurry the hell up, they'd catch her.

Paranoia, how fun.

There was a radio, with fancy-looking buttons. Hannah switched it on but a whine of static met her ears. Off it went. Just her horrible, desperate, strange thoughts for company. Have to think positive, she told herself as she saw lurching shadows from the corners of her eyes. Nothing like the swarms of zombies from her before life, however. An airliner rested on the hill to her left. United. Broken into three pieces, with the weeds and even a tree marking that it had been there a while. No one had come to clean it up. She slowed, as she saw figures emerge from it. Five or so. She sped up when she noticed they all wore uniforms of some kind-- army or marines, perhaps. That they all carried big powerful guns and one even had one pointed at the Mercedes. She went about the corner, her bladder pinging. Please, just let me get somewhere safe, she prayed.

Why had she taken Harrison's car? That was just stupid. It was known, perhaps. Well known, most likely. Why hadn't she pried off the plates or stolen a car or ... not gone on a killing spree? Why had she been so utterly stupid? Why had she cut her wrists? Why not just become a zombie? It seemed like a lot of fun. You wander around, eat and slowly rot! That was kind of like being alive. Hannah wiped at her itchy cheeks; they were wet. Just drive, baby, just drive, she told herself over and over. The wheels yanked her onward. The blacktop needed repairing, but what Idaho road, ever, had been a smooth marvel? She avoided the bigger holes. The cool September morning warmed as she drove along, that sunny sunshine very cheerful. Lucky Peak to her right. Oh.

She stopped, she had to. That once-reservoir had been turned into a churned, unholy mess of chunked concrete, vines and weeds. Something cataclysmic and perhaps even cosmic had happened here. A bomb. A meteor. A war-like act of some kind. An earthquake. Idaho did get earthquakes. Challis, for one. Perhaps Old Faithful had blown, as the doomsayers had been saying before the actual doom had arrived. She watched a zombie, had to be, crawling over the expanse of a halved boulder and then drop down out of sight. What did they eat out here? Did they need to eat or was that just the only memory they had left? The memory of hunger. Of being hungry.

Hannah drove onward, wondering if she should have tried for the Owyhees or even Hells Canyon, up in the corner of Oregon. Perhaps headed toward California, despite whatever had happened that way. Just get out of Boise's shadow. Out of the shadow of her own stupidity. She had the gas card, she had the big powerful important car. She had blankets and coats and a hammer.

Stop it, Hannah. Just keep going somewhat north. You know this country up here a bit, you don't know California or Nevada at all. You've never even been to Hells Canyon. Where are you going to get gas for that? You should have stolen a bicycle and tried to outrace zombies and whatever else.

The road dipped and curved sharply and went upward into the mountains. How many times had she come up here to camp in the trees? At least three times. She had gone camping with the Mortons, their next door neighbors when she and her mother had lived in Caldwell. She and Shawna Morton had shared a tent. The elder Mortons had their own tent, and there had been a big rock-ringed camp fire pit where they had roasted hot dogs and marshmallows, and where Billie Morton had somehow magically made them all some hot chocolate in a sauce pan she had brought from her own kitchen. Elk had called all night. What sounded like a bear had gone by their camp site; something big and grouchy. Deer had run by, so said Mel Morton, when they were enjoying oatmeal and bread toasted over the flames the next morning. "Yes, look," he had pointed at a small pile of black-brown pellets. "That's deer shit."

"Dear," Billie Morton had called out at once, a big plain woman who had gone to the local First Baptist Church far more than necessary. "Dear, little pitchers have big ears."

What good, clean fun that had been. Shawna had been a genuinely nice girl, her parents had been genuinely nice people. Which was rather rare in this bitchkitty of a world. What had happened to them? Were they here somewhere in this messed up otherworld? Otherworld, yes, that was the name for this reality or plane, whatever it was. Hell, perhaps. Maybe the Mortons toiled somewhere in Region Five, pretending all of this was normal. Pretending as hard as possible. She hoped her mother, who had died of a massive sudden heart attack when Hannah had been twenty-two, remained decently dead and not a part of any of this. Oh she hoped so, with all that was left of her heart. She drove onward, at something above a snail's pace.

The road got worse. The mountains seemed chewed by giants. Big chunks had been removed or blasted away. Mining could do that—they had mined the shit out of

Idaho at one time. Gold, semi-precious gems, silver. The mines had dried up or had grown too expensive to keep going. But yes, mines could have ruined these wild Idaho places easily, in moments. But she doubted mining operations had taken half a hillside, leaving behind a yawning crater that nature had only just tried, lately, to cover with a bit of green. Some battle had been waged here. She went around a corner, the creek to her right. Morgan Creek. Where was Rebel Creek? Had she made that up? A deer flashed across the road, chased by, yes, a pack of slinky wolves. Hannah let the pursuing predators pass by, her head turned to watch the ancient dance of death and life. If there were deer running about and wolves ... then there wouldn't be a ton of zombies or even other people about up here. Or maybe the deer and wolves had been a mirage, just something she wished to see. A sign to let her know she would live a somewhat happy life in some barricaded cabin...

Something hit the Mercedes and the car rocked on its tires. Hannah started, looked to the passenger side where, yes, a zombie peered in at her. This one looked very lively. Dark skin, gummy eyes, all of its teeth as they were bared at her. The fingers scrabbled at the door handle and she heard the door click open.

"Fuck you," she said, leaning over to yank that door closed even as she hit the all-lock button on her door panel. She flipped the zombie off as it tried to get in, as it gibbered at her, as actual words dribbled from those scaled back lips.

"Come out girlie, smell you, smell good, hungry."

A monotonous moan of mostly how hungry it was and that she smelled good. It came around to the driver side. The stench of zombie flesh.

Why am I sitting here? Hannah wondered as she put the

car into drive and continued her journey. That zombie shambled after her and then she saw those wolves surround it. Hannah stopped to watch the wolves go after that zombie. Five wolves, in a near ring, quick and slim, seeming to smile at the prey that had wandered into their territory. They tore the lively zombie to pieces, just yanked it apart with a few vicious renderings. The zombie killed a wolf. Ripped the head off, drank the blood even as the other wolves closed in. The wolves dragged that zombie off the road. Would they become zombie wolves if they ate zombie flesh? Probably not. Something about being bitten or maybe just some sort of evil magic made one a zombie. So the local bad ass predators took care of the zombie menaces. Hannah smiled, her mind drifting into a soft gray place. She floated there for quite some time before noticing that the wolves had crept toward her stopped car; that they watched and waited to see what she would do. She drove onward. No more of that going off where she had no thoughts at all, it would get her killed. Time to survive. It was time to survive.

For several miles, perhaps even ten or more, she drove onward. The gas gauge seemed to drift toward empty a bit fast. The sky had that thin clear look, which summer skies did not. Winter, winter, winter! It would arrive. Snow and ice, the gods of death. She drove onward, the only vehicle so far. She drove onward.

Until Highway 21 just ended. A giant crater yawned before Hannah. Impassable even with a four wheel drive. She took the gun out of the glove box, flipped the safety off, got out of the car, and found the air smelling of pine trees. Water nearby. Water far far far below. This giant crater had not been here in that other time she knew and remembered. The road continued rather mockingly on the far, other side of that crater. Her eyes told her it had to be half a mile across. Driving around it was not an option. She could try to haul everything, on her back or carry it, around that deep hole or ... turn around and try something else.

Maybe Highway 55 was still open? Probably not. Even in good times, it had been a nightmare of landslides, blizzards, accidents and road construction delays. Head towards Mountain Home or try to get to Jackpot, Nevada? Try to reach Eastern Oregon, except that way seemed extra messed up. Or maybe not. Maybe that was all lies. Maybe it was great there and people lived in harmony and peace and good fellowship. No one had to know she'd murdered two humans and one zombie overlord guy. No sir!

Down below. There was water. She could build a shelter. Out of what? And it would have to repel wolves, bears, cougars and zombies. And probably other people that came across her as well. People were truly shits, she had learned that one the very hard way. But if she somehow managed to build a fort below, she could hike back into Boise for supplies. Oh yes, just march into Shopper's World and charge a bunch of crap to Harrison's account. A hold up. A robbery, then. And then deal with the new version of the Boise PD. If they caught her, of course.

How had she come to this mess?

Oh yes, she had been utterly stupid. Perhaps in a book or bad Hollywood blockbuster, she would be delivered into some far better place where everything would be okay. Reality seemed far different than movies sprinkled with monsters and superheroes and screamy, bitchy girlfriends who told the heroes to be careful a lot. She'd love to stand to one side and tell some square-jawed sort to be careful while he took on the zombie menaces. And then the zombies could eat her after they were done unzipping the hero's guts and sucking out the contents. And she could scream and scream and not get saved at all.

"Pull it together, Hannah," she told herself. A rustle to her left. A man in a soldier's camouflage stood there. He put his finger to his soft, puffy beestung lips, his dark eyes as mad and empty as the eyes of a doll. He held a sword, but the gun shops sold swords and the military would have them in abundance. A black man, with a shimmering bald head.

"Watch out for the wolves," this military man told her in a low whisper of a voice. His eyes slid all over her but not in a sleazy or awful way. His eyes went to the car, to the big crevasse, to the other side of that big crevasse, to the trees and bushes, back to her, over and over and over. It became rather unnerving. He sniffed toward her, she understood why.

"Okay," she said and he nodded. "Do you know what happened here?"

"Wolves," he replied. He had begun to back away. "We're gonna build a wall. This is part of the wall. Wolves all over. Wolves. Wall building keeps us busy. Wolves, ma'am."

"Wolves did that? Great." She knew that small pack of wolves was not that far away. But they would be full from deer and zombie. Wolves, as far as she knew, were not idiotically destructive. They were not humans, after all. Humans destroyed everything they touched. Wolves did not. It was really that awful, terrible and simple.

"Human wolves," the military man added, peering down now as a zombie wandered across the broken and crumbled ground far below. "You be careful, lady. You be careful. You put something cold on that face." His fingers oh so gently ran over her cheek. "You're real and you're dead. This isn't the world. This isn't the world, right? You be careful." His hand fell away, his eyes filled with sense, with something like knowledge.

"Too late for that," she said.

Tears rolled down his coffee-colored cheeks, the blank mad eyes just produced tears over the fate of Highway 21 and perhaps the fate of everything on the planet. Her hand reached out, she had no notion she would try to take his loosely curled hand, the one not holding the sword. The man shied away. "I'm sorry." Everything wanted to bubble out of her; the last two days, everything, everything. Her throat closed instead.

"Me, too," he whispered, and then flung himself over that edge before she knew what was what. He fell, he fell through the air, straight down and she had to watch. He lay where he ended up, not moving for a long time. His legs looked all wrong, probably broken on impact. And he had not taken his sword. It lay on the pavement. Throwing it down to him seemed pointless. Oh dear, was she making jokes while watching a man commit a long, slow suicide? Yes. Yes, she was. The zombie ambled toward the jumper and she had to watch, she had to.

They fought and the zombie won, as simple and elemental as that. The zombie bent over the dead man, to feed. And then she noticed the wolves had come after all. They came like ghosts out of the brush and rocks so far below. Like ghosts. Perhaps they had come to pay their respects to that military man. The zombie fled from the wolves and they chased him away, and the dead man lay there, far below, very dead. How soon before she just gave up and leaped off the nearest cliff? Very soon. Very soon.

She had already cut her wrists.

The memory of that remained fresh and vivid. If there's one zombie or one wolf, she considered, there's others.

Hannah got back into the Mercedes, and got it turned around and pointed back at Boise. She turned the engine off and just sat there. A bird trilled. A hawk swooped in that big empty sky. Night would be here in a bit. It was almost October. She had a half a tank of gas. The Mercedes did not seem that environmentally friendly. Why would they still have cars that ran on gasoline in a world overrun by banker zombies? Who worked the oil fields? Who refined the oil? Were the fossil fuel big boys still up and running even now? Their days had been drawing to a close in the world she had known. Perhaps they had loosed all of this onto planet earth to keep the money flowing in. You needed tanks and fighter planes to fight zombies. And such things ran on gas and diesel. Hannah had to smile at finding herself forming conspiracy theories worthy of the most far left radical commie hippie ever invented by Idaho's conservative fringies. Lyle would be so proud of her for finally waking up. A crackpot invented by other crackpots to convince... Her smile faded.

PART TWENTY-TWO: OPTIONS

Her options. Go back to Harry's house and hope no one noticed she'd set it on fire and killed everyone in it. She could live there, after the fire was put out. Keep calling into the office that Harry was sick! Use his credit cards and whatever money he had there. Hadn't there been an old movie about three secretaries holding their boss hostage or killing their boss and then trying to make it look like he was still alive? Had they been found out or had they gotten away with it? No. Going back toward Boise would just get her killed. She turned her head to the left. A zombie peered in at her, with half the face gone. An oddly clear, very blue eye peered in at her, the other eye had rotted and oozed out of the bare bone socket. How was that thing still walking around? This was some form of souped up rabies? That kept you somehow walking around and yet rotting and wanting brains and flesh?

It knocked on the window. "Hey. Wanna?" It winked at her, crooked a peeled finger at her, an invitation. *To what? Play Monopoly?*

Hannah drove away from that crater, with the zombie shambling after her in the usual fashion. Except it kept up with the car for quite a while before it fell away. Had it been a runner before? She slowed as she caught sight of a tiny, rutted dirt road leading up and around the hill to her right. Morgan Creek Loop. She'd never heard of it but she had not come up this way very often. It looked okay. A bit washed out and full of pot holes from hell, but the Mercedes dipped and lurched obediently onward, like a tired horse used by tourists to tour the Grand Canyon. Or had they used mules? Did the Grand Canyon even exist anymore? Boxes, supplies, foodstuffs slewed and slid as she guided that big, heavy car up and up, around the twisty little bends, beneath the leaning pine trees that would remain somewhat green even in deep winter.

"Where are you going?"

Her own voice startled her. Rocks scraped the undercarriage: *scriiiitch screeetch.* Shadows held hands among the trees and tried to trick her eyes. She noted if she had to go back to the main highway, she'd have to do that in reverse. Place to turn around? Not available so far. Just the narrowing road and the unforgiving trees.

Hannah, stop. Back up. There's nothing up here.

She kept climbing steadily up. She splashed through tiny streams that meandered across the narrow road that was edged with trees and shaggy bushes.

If you run out of gas up here, there's no help.

I can help myself, she answered herself with real amusement and actual despair.

The front left tire suddenly plunged into an innocent looking bit of the road. She barely kept the Mercedes from slamming into the nearest grouping of grim trees. A small bit of stream ran across the road, right beneath her front end. She got that hammer, and got out of the car. Just birds, the call of crickets; no groans, gibberings or shots ringing out.

Reverse. Go back. Try going forward. Do something, Hannah.

She set her lips into a thin line, then tasted that stream water from her cupped hand. She spat it out. It tasted rancid, full of chemicals, even as clear and sparkly as it ran over the smooth rocks fitted with dull red strands of water moss. The water needed to be boiled, that was all. Hannah got back in the car, her skin suddenly prickling. Had that been a growl? Five elk suddenly bounded across the narrowing dirt road; big astonishing animals. Two with big racks, three without, all spooked. Dogs. Dogs chasing them. Perhaps they had been pets, but hadn't this world or plane been like this for fifty years?

I'm in the future, this is the future... How did I get here? What is the meaning of life? I'm walking here!

The dogs snarled and nipped at each other, like the wolves had, but they seemed clumsy and strange here, and the wolves had seemed to fit. A German Shepherd, a Labrador, and several mixed breeds, all after those elk with such hungry ineptness.

Hannah sat in the car long after that strange procession had passed by. She put the car in reverse and the wheel spun uselessly in that silt, mud and muck. She tried going forward, gunning the engine until it screamed and surely alerted everything within a hundred miles to come and get her. And then turned the car off. Listened to the cooling engine as it ticked and ticked, as steam rose gently from underneath that dark blue hood. The little narrow dirt road, which had tufts of grass growing in between the tracks this far up, continued on the other side of that demon stream. It bent sharply to the left, so she could no longer see what lay ahead. Oh no, that would be too easy. There was water here. She could use the car as a shelter until she got something built. She had food. She had matches. Boise and all that was not far enough away. That she could remedy if she survived the winter. She got out, then hastily got back in. Those dogs had returned for far easier prey. "No." Hannah got the gun. She had some shots left. She got that hammer ready. Rolling the window down, she shot three dogs: all the ammunition she had. That left six dogs. They kept away, leery skinny ghosts that had perhaps once been pets. Or had been born in this new world where pets were the humans kept by zombies for amusement, sex and eventually, food.

Hannah tried to reverse. That engine sounded choppy now and her gas gauge had swung to just above the red. The car dipped even further downward.

Stop, Hannah, you're making it worse. Stop. When those dogs leave, and they will, you can get out, get something under that tire and then get the hell out of here.

Had her little voices ever steered her wrong? No, they had not. She waited, in the steadily heating interior of that Mercedes, her throat drying up. To be back in that shitty apartment, with taps that worked. With that shower that worked.

And the rest of it? The rest of it, Hannah?

She touched the button to roll down the window. It barely responded. She had messed up the engine. The dogs drew closer, panting, eager to make her their next meal. Maybe they thought she was a zombie. She could not get that window to go back up. No. No!

The German Shepherd, with nothing in its amber eyes but murder, leaped at her, snarling, big teeth bared and ready to rip out her throat. She whacked it with the hammer. It fell back, screaming that canine scream that so hurt her. No dog should scream like that, no matter what it had done. The other dogs kept back. The German Shepherd shook its long head, and probably had a headache to go with that blood she had drawn in her hasty whacking.

"I am not being killed by a pack of dogs while trapped in this car," she told that pack of dogs. They snarled at her that yes, that was exactly what would happen.

Everything had been put in the capacious trunk. What did she have in the backseat? Water, for instance? Blankets? It would get cold up here. Far colder than down below in the Treasure Valley, once called the Snake River

Valley. Her mother had told her that. And something else before that, by the Shoshone or Paiute or Bannon or Nez Perce. Her mind had thrown out those names slick as shit.

PART TWENTY-THREE: THAT'S LIFE, BABY

Two days.

She tried the door but no dog slyly guarding from the bunching trees came snarling toward her. Snow splattered the mushy ground and the sky looked solid with snow clouds. It snowed early in snow country — oh yes, it did. Hannah shivered in that still, cool air. Had the dogs moved on? The three she had shot had been dragged away or just casually eaten by the other dogs. But no zombies had come through. The Mercedes now seemed permanently mired. The stream had risen a bit, it touched the bumper now. Scratches on the midnight blue paint job; sorry, Harry. She kneeled by that demonic stream, the miniature stream, and took a drink. Let it kill her. Better than crouching in a car, waiting. Her stomach rumbled then settled. She had gotten used to dirty water. The shits would arrive, maybe kill her.

That's life, baby, that's life. Sorry for peeing in the back seat and pooing there as well, Harry!

Her mind seemed full of cottonballs and candy. Enough of that. Time to scout the area. Time to start living, instead of waiting to die. She took the keys and opened the trunk. Took a can of ravioli, bashed it open, no can opener, and ate the contents. Slimy, tasteless. Food.

Explore the area. Find a shelter. Get it fortified. Get to work, Hannah.

Hannah took her magical hammer. It had begun to seem a bit magical and all-powerful, which was dangerous and idiotic thing to to think, but it helped her mood. She took a moment to, yes, do a number two, as her mother so coyly used to say. It would firm up. Or she would shit herself to death. She went onward, following that road, listening, listening. The further she got from the mired, dead Mercedes, the jumpier she got.

Jumpy will keep me alive. Jumpy is good!

She came to that sharp bend and looked down into a sort of valley, with a house and small buildings here and there.

Her eyes took in that no smoke rose from the chimney. Her eyes took in no one seemed to live there. No movement. The big four wheel drive seemed to be sitting on four flats. She could change a tire, if there were four tires available. Even jump a dead battery, but she'd need jumper cables and a good battery for that. A clearing with someone's retirement home, built away from everyone else. Where were the folks who lived here? Hannah noted the road went sharply down, then wandered by that place and toward what looked like a small river — perhaps even Morgan Creek itself.

Go down there, Hannah. Get moving.

Another bout with her bowels, then she did get moving.

The closer she got, the more deserted it looked. Windows broken. That chimney looked a bit like it leaned. Yes, it did. The vehicle did indeed sit on four flats, and had a big dent in its once-shiny side. Dust had covered it. Dark green with strange District Five plates. GMC. Where did they still make cars in zombie banker America? Hannah listened very hard, but she heard nothing that alarmed her. Birds. Something small running through the tall sere grasses. She sensed no eyes on her, she could not smell that high stink of zombie. The house itself had been built of big logs and plywood sheets, and had a tin roof. Rustic would probably figure in the realtor's description of this one. Just a big square house, with two layers. The curtains at the windows were either pulled back or hung half off their rods. The porch had a big hole punched in it and a raccoon chittered at her as she peered down into that hole. Chipmunks scolded her and scattered to the four winds as she actually tried the door, which was locked. She went around back and that door had come off its hinges a bit. Nobody lived here. Not for years perhaps. She could see zombies and wolves and dog packs coming and could defend herself, could build defenses and traps. Lyle had shown her how to build a bow and how to make arrows. She didn't need a gun; they were too noisy, and what could she make ammo out of anyway? A hand pump with a spout and a bucket nearby. Old-fashioned in these new-fangled times. Her mind stored that hand pump. She also noted a broken down windmill. Had she wandered into some prepper's last stand against zombie-fication?

Hannah eased that backdoor to the side and peeked into the house. A big kitchen, a living room beyond that, stairs going upward. Simple.

"Hello?" Her voice caused mice to scatter. They had chewed everything to pieces. The end tables could be used for kindling. The two chairs needed tossed. No kitchen table? Ah, trays. The folks here had eaten off TV trays. The couch looked destroyed, a big leather number. Who had dragged that beast up here? The curtains — dark green — hung like limp surrender flags.

Upstairs she found two bedrooms, one had been used for storage. The mattress would have to be replaced. Two long-dead people lay on it, their heads blown to smithereens. What a smithereen was escaped Hannah, as she stared at the two who had done as she had done with a bit of broken glass. Except they had used an old shotgun, which lay on the floor, covered with dust. Both chambers empty. The casings had fallen to the floor. Two women. Mother and daughter? Lovers? Sisters? Hannah stepped out of the bedroom. She had no blame for the two. Or condemnation or pity. They had done as they had seen fit and that was that. They might even have been passing through and decided to remain here forever in this tiny valley. Things had been nibbling at them and their brains had dried to weird streaks on the bedroom wall.

A mattress could be made from a sleeping bag stuffed with something. A sack stuffed with hay. Or the cleaner stuffing leaking from that beast of a couch.

Time to get back to practical matters, Hannah.

The fireplace had a stack of wood beside it, crumbly, chewed, covered with little hard mouse pellets. There were also vents in the wooden floors, but the light switches did not turn the lights on and off. Candles. She saw candles, long unlit, waiting for matches. She tried the tap in the kitchen. Nothing. Books, grown dusty. The Bible. The Fountainhead by Ayn Rand. Truth for Our Times by Chester Fighter. 100 Ways to Cook Wild Game by Suzimarie Crockett. Excellent. God, some book she'd never heard of, some political screaming, and recipes for chipmunk balls and homemade noodles. At least that last book might come in useful. The other books could be used to start fires, if it came down to it. Had these few books belonged to the two women or someone else?

She went back out, checking the area—a habit she had learned. The hand pump, after several cranks, gushed forth water. She tasted it. Cold, hard, clean-tasting. Gathered underground when the snow melted, perhaps. And, if this water dried up, she had the little river nearby. She could even hear it. It would be a long haul to get water to the house. Was she already moved in and comfy here?

Water. Food could be mice, raccoons and feral dogs. And deer and elk. If she could bring one down. She had shelter. She'd be too busy trying to stay alive to worry about being bored or if she wanted or needed company. Clothes. Well… She'd deal with that. She'd deal with everything. Everything in that Mercedes needed to be carried here to her new house. She also needed to build or dig a hidey-hole in case of company or attacks. A place to retreat, to wait out the threat. Oh, so much work to be done here. Clean that house, scout the area further. She might well be too close to some zombie military outpost or something like that.

She hauled the two women out of the house and shut them up in the tiny tool shed, after she had removed a hatchet, another hammer, a can of nails, some cord, a shovel, a big pile of rope, a pair of pliers, a big axe, a whetstone, and a box of shotgun shells. Noisy, but waving a gun at others seemed more effective than waving a hatchet.

PART TWENTY-FOUR: CAST IRON AND STONES

Time passed, winter arrived. Spring showed up late. Hannah survived—barely so, but she survived. She cut off her hair, she let the hair on her legs and under her arms flourish. She hid from the few wandering zombies. She grew thin and hard and silent. Her stomach seemed made of cast iron and thorns. She ate whatever she could catch, run down, or shoot at with her badly made bow and steadily improving arrows. She dug up cattail roots. Dandelions proved tasty. The two moldering women in the tool shed had planted a small garden. Squash she had, but no wheat or corn. She saved the seeds. Hannah promised herself she'd bury those two when she got a moment. She promised that with a straight face. She went over that useful, practical cookbook until she wore it to tatters. Illustrations of edible plants.

Another winter. Another. The dogs came through on occasion. Wolves skittered through but they had enough to eat. No helicopters or planes went overhead and she did not hear any other motors. She had dug herself a sort of underground fort, reinforced with boards she had taken from here and there. The cookbook had even told how to make pemmican, in the Shoshone fashion. Dried and pounded meat, berries, nuts, fat. Add a pinch of salt. She'd have to hike out to get salt. Or coffee. Or tea. She had water, which she could boil and add mint or pine needles to. No sugar. She cooked over the fireplace. She worked. She survived.

Winter again. Hannah coughed long and hard, and there, on her palm, blood. She curled up in her nest of old ratty blankets and barely cured elk hide. The fire crackled. Had she ever been so damn tired? She coughed for a long time, unable to catch her breath.

I'm a pioneer now, she thought, smiling even as she coughed and choked and coughed. *I should die of some pioneer disease.*

Those fish she had drying needed to be checked. She had to redo the wall around the garden for next spring. She needed to make sure the roof… Something about the roof. Her chest burned and ached, her breath would not come and go easy. Hannah curled up, smelling the odor of her bedding, feeling the hard floor beneath her thin homemade mattress. She lived next to that fireplace. Being trapped upstairs — no thanks.

I don't mind dying this way, she told God and Happy Jesus and the devil. *I don't mind at all.*

Happy. She had grown happy here. The fire crackled and spat. Snowing, it was snowing, she could hear it. She heard wind chimes. The world had heated up, she threw aside her ratty blankets.

"I'd like a cup of coffee. With cream and sugar. And some Twizzlers." She laughed and coughed, laughed and coughed. The night swallowed her and she went, she went so gladly. Let her have served whatever sentence this was. Let her go on to that place of many mansions. What a thought, that she'd have her own room in heaven. Would they let her decorate it? A mouse ran over her.

I need to bury those two out in that damn shed. A mouse nibbled at her foot. *No hobo clown broken glass for me.* The night and the snow and the crackle of that fire.

PART TWENTY-FIVE: WIND CHIMES AND MOLLY

A wet dog's tongue. The panting breath of an anxious canine. Hannah's fingers gripped short fur, oily slick and soft. That swift slap of that same tongue, the suppressed bark that sounded like a question. *What's wrong, human? What's wrong?* Hannah opened her eyes, her hand going to her face. She had just been coughing herself to death in a shack.

Hannah sat on a porch that had seen better days. A wind chime someone had made from old flattened tin spoons clanked musically in the wind that rushed through now and then. A big clay pot that held a cherry tomato plant that had seen better days, poor thing. A big elm tree and a cottonwood fighting for dominance in the overgrown lawn that needed mowing. The sounds of people laughing in the house at her back. Or was that a television playing? A television. So normal. It was so normal here, wherever this was.

She sat in a splintery wooden lawn chair, her lap full of a shirt, the index and thumb of her right hand holding a sewing needle, threaded with black thread. The shirt in her lap seemed to need mending and she had been in the act of mending it while sitting outside on a nice late morning. Maybe it was afternoon. Maybe it was not a time at all, just a dream or a fancy. Spring or early summer. It had that feel of nice weather and pleasant nights, before it turned so ghastly hot and dry. She wore a short-sleeved red blouse over stretchy dark gray pants with bleach spots on the lower legs. No shoes, her toenails painted with bright pink polish. When had she painted her toenails?

Zombie apocalypse — ah, can't go scavenging until my toenails look good! Hannah wiggled those decorated tootsies, wiggled them and wiggled them.

Hannah stuck the needle in the black and red plaid shirt, noting the sleeve had become separated a bit from the shoulder. She could barely sew but she could fix a rip or tear, so holding a needle did not feel that strange. Her surroundings did not seem familiar, yet they did. Was this still Idaho? She eyed the dog, who trotted back out to the lawn, and came back with a stick. A yellow Labrador wearing a faded pink collar. A healthy, well-fed, beloved Lab, at that. Who seemed to know her. A man stepped out of the house, bare-foot, with overgrown man toenails on display, in old jeans. He had black hair — springy and somewhat curly. His eyes crinkling as she looked up at him, as she struggled not to give an actual real scream at the sight of Harrison Squack, who held a peeled onion in his hand and a knife in the other. His eyes. A clear brownish-green. Not the muddy ruin of zombie eyeballs.

"Molly! Good girl," he said and then he threw that stick for the excitable dog; a clean long throw, the stick tumbling over and over, rather like she had been tumbling just a bit ago. The dog raced beneath that stick with a happy chorus of barks. "You don't have to do that, Han. You okay? You seem tired." He even bent and kissed the top of her head. And then Salliana peeked out, wearing a hoodie, very baggy sweat pants and a sullen cast to her face, a careful wariness. Her black hair in a braid that snaked over her skinny shoulder. She had a tattoo on her throat, barbed wire. Kids these days.

"Salli and I are trying to make dinner. Tacos. She wanted tacos. We finally found the taco seasoning. You'd put it in the freezer for some reason. Did you hear us laughing?"

"I like tacos, so sue me," Salliana muttered, in such an expected teenager fashion, but her eyes held light in them. Harrison punched her arm: a light, affectionate tap of his knuckles against Salli's bicep. She tossed that hoodie-covered head, but a smile raced across those sullen lips.

I'm not old enough to be her mother, thought Hannah in actual alarm and even realer indignation. He gave the young girl the onion and knife. Salliana went back inside and Harrison threw the stick for the dog, Molly, again, smiling as Molly raced after it with the tireless devotion of a zealot.

"Is this Idaho?" Hannah had to ask. *I do know this house, I do know those wind chimes. Where is this?* Where were the zombies? Had the zombie evolved back into real people? How would she die here and where would she go next? Her eyes grew wet, stung as if someone had rubbed an ocean of salt in the raw meat of her face. Her fish. Her fish could rot. She had worked so hard to catch them. Her seeds would dry up, they would not get planted if she was not there. *I'm crazy. This is what crazy is.*

"Last time I checked. She started talking today, you notice? She's been so withdrawn and afraid, but today she said she wanted tacos. I think we're really helping her." Harrison pulled up a folding chair that had been placed on this warped-boarded porch, with two fragile wooden steps leading down to the yard. "Did you hear? More people got attacked. Now they're saying it's some weird virus that makes you aggressive. Some form of mutant rabies. Rabies isn't bad enough? Some world, huh. I don't know. I guess I should go grate some cheese, but it's such a nice afternoon. Good girl, Molly! Who's the best girl ever?" Harrison threw the stick again. Birds twittered and fought in the elm and cottonwood. The cottonwood released its snowflake-like spore into the air, it drifted past her, it drifted past her as she listened to Salliana chopping that onion in the kitchen. An airplane lumbered through the sky. She heard traffic, the rumble of a tractor's engine. "You got the early shift at Target tomorrow?" His hand curled through her limp one. He smelled alive. One of those tall, skinny, spider-limbed men that never put on weight. She had watched this man eat a cat named Pebbles. She had watched that. "Hannah? Honey? Why are you crying? Honey."

His arm slipped about her shoulders, just like something out of the movies. It was not any more real than the movies. There was the heat of that arm about her, there was his voice like a cough drop, something soothing and tasting of medicine and mint. She tasted that voice of his in her throat. Raw pennies underneath it, that hint of blood. A cough drop made with blood. Hannah looked away from Harrison, waiting. Alert. Looking for a weapon. Hannah refused to repeat her list of stupid ass mistakes this time around, and next time around, and the time after that, damn it. She heard Salliana in the kitchen nearby, that knife hitting a cutting board.

"It's zombies, the world is about to be eaten by zombies," Hannah said, turning to Harrison. He patted her arm, smiled at her, gave a small laugh and then threw the stick for delighted Molly again, and again after that, and again after that.

ABOUT THE AUTHOR

Ann Wuehler is a native of Oregonian with ambitions and apparently a need to see more of the planet than a few feet beyond her back yard. Ann received her BA in Theatre from Eastern Oregon University and her MFA in Playwriting from the University of Nevada/Las Vegas. Anne has had plays done from as far as field as Iceland to Australia and has been published, in Ten, Ten Minute Plays Volume 2 and 3-- the Next Mrs. Jacob Anderson and the Care and Feeding of Baby Birds.

Ann's Oregon Gothic, a collection of short stories, was published in 2015. Her House on Clark Boulevard, a novel, was published September of 2017. She had an evening of plays September 2018 with the Ilkley Playhouse in the UK. Her third novel, Aftermath: Boise, Idaho, will be out around Halloween of 2020. The Sun published her Mouse and Man short story in the April 2020 edition. Twisted Vine published her Imptown for its spring 2020 edition. The Santa Ana River Review published her short play, The Bluegrass of God, this year as well. Whistle Pig will publish her short story, Greenhorn, for their 12th edition. Her short play, Traces of Memory, will be made into a brief film by filmmakers in Los Angeles and by a director from the Czech Republic. Death Rattle's Oroboro published her flash fiction piece, Vineheart and the Stolen Daughters. The Ghastling included her short story, The Little Visitors, in their Book Ten. Ann is also co-writing a screenplay, entitled Prince Charming, based on a short story from her Oregon Gothic collection,with Lucie Gerkkertova. She is super-excited to be a member of Poe Boy Publishing.

MORE BOOKS BY THE PUBLISHER

GHOST HUNTER Z BY D.A. SCHNEIDER

London, 1883. The American only known as Z has made a new home in the great city. However, Z is not like other men. Since he was just a boy, he's had the ability to see ghosts. Though the gift frightened him at first, he soon learned to live with it, and more, start his own business as a ghost hunter, ridding haunted houses of their restless spirits. Fleeing a horrifying past in the States, Z crossed the pond with his silver loaded revolvers on his hips and Stetson hat on his head, determined to hunt and fight the supernatural.

When Scotland Yard Inspector Charles Grant approaches Z with a job, the case pits the ghost hunter against an ancient evil. Asmodeus is coming and he brings an army of demons with him. Now, Grant must find the murderer who spilled human blood to summon the King of Demons, while Z races to find the one object that can drive the evil back to Hell. But will Z's past catch up to him first?

AMAZON UK:

https://amzn.to/2Z9L5I0

AMAZON USA:

https://amzn.to/2BJTzh5

The Nightmare Tree (Ghost Hunter Z Book 2)

Young Jeffery is an orphan with a special gift. He can see ghosts. When the boy is abducted, Ghost Hunter Z is recruited to find him, surprised to find another that shares his talent. The hunt will lead him and his new associate Rudder Wallace to The Nightmare Tree, a realm populated by twisted creatures and an ancient deity intent on keeping the boy right where he is. Meanwhile, Inspector Grant is on the case, following clues to find the kidnapper. The evidence leads him and the rest of the team to a new threat in the form of a skilled magic user that's willing to perform unspeakable acts out of desperation. What sinister plot has been set in motion? And who is pulling the strings from behind the scenes? Before Z can discover the truth, he must first survive The Nightmare Tree.

AMAZON UK:
https://amzn.to/39kmANj

AMAZON USA:
https://amzn.to/2Bc8UqX

THE STAFF OF SET GHOST HUNTER Z BOOK 3

Seether's mad quest to recover the pieces to complete the Staff of Set are coming closer to fruition. Now, Ghost Hunter Z and his team race to find the final artifact first, a mission that leads half the team on a challenging trip by ship to Egypt. Meanwhile, Z and his friends are being targeted by a mad man with the ability to control fire. Inspector Grant is on the hunt to find the killer before he can strike again. Twists and shocking surprises await all members of the team in this thrilling conclusion to The Ghost Hunter Z Trilogy.

AMAZON UK:
https://amzn.to/30Nz7FK

AMAZON USA:
https://amzn.to/34Mvtgq

THE 9 GHOSTS OF SAMEN'S BANE

The only constant in life is death.
For Adrian Dillard, death has become an unwelcome
companion. Nine unwelcome companions to be exact.
Killed in a tragic train derailment over century ago, the
ghosts of nine children have taken up residence in
Adrian's psyche. Using him as a conduit for their
incredible abilities, Adrian is put through arduous
training to face off against The Nine's ancient enemy
Samen, Lord of Evil Spirits. But Adrian knows he isn't
being told the full story. Soon, the dead children seem to
have other motives, and the appearance of other
supernatural creatures calls everything Adrian has
learned in to doubt. He must uncover the truth behind it
all and try to avoid death trying.

AMAZON UK:
https://amzn.to/2YW060c

AMAZON USA:
https://amzn.to/2YOPRuw

THE MOST BORING MAN IN THE WORLD – BY WEE GEORDIE NUMPTY

The Most Boring Man In The World by Wee Geordie Numpty is a unique at times hilarious look at boredom and being bored with modern life.

We've all be bored at some point in life, especially in 2020 - The Most Boring Man in The World takes boredom to a whole new level.

"This book is so boring it's riveting!"

The Second most boring man in the world.

AMAZON UK:

https://amzn.to/3eBcJnY

AMAZON USA:

https://amzn.to/3eBxcJp